I hope you enj

Cindy Kline

To David and Ethan. I couldn't have done this without your love and support.

To James Herbert - thank you for being you!

Chapter 1

The engines of the 757 airplane drummed below my seat as I held my breath. My death grip on the armrests turning my knuckles white as the plane ascended. My ears plugged, muting the murmurs of passengers around me. I took a series of deep breaths, letting them out slowly. I could do this. A minute later, the plane leveled out, and I loosened my grip, flexing my cramped fingers.

"Are you okay, lass?"

My head turned toward the deep, Irish accent. I vaguely recalled someone sitting down next to me, but had paid little attention. I was too busy convincing my stomach to stay where it was and not end up in my throat.

Looking at him now, he might have been an equally sufficient diversion. I would guess late thirties, maybe early forties. His eyes were the same shade as Lake Huron on a bright sunny day, what my cousin would call cobalt blue. His hair was dark and curly, just reaching the collar of his shirt, and it was thick—the type women like to run their fingers through. He had an athletic build, the muscles in his arms noticeable through the light sweater he wore over a collared shirt.

I tried to smile, but it came out more like a grimace as my stomach slowly crawled back to where it belonged. "I'm fine. Well, now, anyway. I'm not a good flyer. It's not that I think the plane is going to crash or anything. I can't ride Ferris wheels either. It's a vertigo thing." I looked at the grin on his face. "And now I'm babbling, giving you way more information that you asked for. Sorry—it's a bad habit of mine when I'm nervous."

He smiled, showing off his white teeth and almost perfect smile. There was one tooth overlapping, but it didn't detract from his pleasant looks. "I enjoy a woman who tells the truth, even if it does require listening to the babble." He leaned his head into the aisle and lifted his hand, "Miss?"

The flight attendant walked toward us from the front of the plane. The leggy brunette placed her hand on his shoulder and asked with a soft smile, "What can I do for you, sir?"

"May I have a scotch and water, and a brandy for my seatmate."

"My pleasure, sir."

"Oh, I don't need—" I tried to say.

"Heed my advice. Yes, you do."

"Are you an expert on babbling?"

"Let's just say I've had plenty of training, including an ex-wife and a teenage daughter."

"If you don't mind my asking, what is it you do?" I could imagine him working in construction, or leaping tall buildings in a single bound.

"I have a boring job with the Irish government."

"You're too tan to work behind a desk."

He chuckled. "I'm returning home from holiday in California. Ever been there?"

"Unfortunately, I've not been farther west than Wisconsin. Why California?

"You'll probably find this strange, but I went to visit my ex-in-laws." He chuckled.

"Not really. Just because you're divorced from their daughter doesn't mean you have to cut her parents out of your life. I, however, detest my soon-to-be ex-in-laws and will be keeping a great distance."

His eyes widened. "You're the first person who hasn't told me I'm a muppet."

I smiled. "No, you're not a fool, and it's been a long time since I've heard that term."

"You sound like you're from Ireland, but you have a wee bit of Yank in you. How come?"

"Born and bred in Ireland, but moved to America a little over five years ago to get married." I looked down at the bare ring finger on my left hand and then glanced at him. He was looking at the bare finger also.

"Coming back for a visit?"

"Moving back, actually. I've been living in Michigan, but since my husband and I split up, well, there's no reason for me to stay." I blinked back the tears threatening to fall. "Definitely not where I thought I would be at this point in my life."

"I'm sorry to hear that. I know from experience divorce is tough."

"Mine will be final in three months." I let my breath out slowly. When will this weight of failure go away? It's like a giant squid clinging to my back, sucking the life out of me. "Was your divorce amicable?"

He looked downcast, tapping his fingers on his leg. "Yes, surprisingly. But Tiffany had wanted out for a while. It took me longer to realize she'd left the marriage a long time ago, and it was wise for me to get on with my life."

"How long has it been since you've been divorced?" I shifted in my seat to get more comfortable.

"Just over a year now. I know this sounds like a cliché, but it does get easier," he grinned.

I nodded. It was a cliché, but hopefully, one that was valid. "Do you have any children?" I could imagine a little boy with dark hair and those penetrating eyes running around, causing mischief.

His smile widened. "One. A daughter attending Trinity College. She has one more year to go."

The flight attendant appeared just then with a tray. We both pulled our tables out from the armrests, and she set down a napkin on each, then our drinks, never taking her eyes off the man next to me. I tried to hide my smile, but it didn't work. He looked at me, saw my grin, and grinned back.

"Sláinte," he said as he lifted his glass to me.

I lifted my glass to him as well. "Sláinte," I took a sip of the amber liquid. It burned as it hit my throat but was warm the rest of the way down.

The flight attendant was clearly interested in him, but he was either clueless or didn't care, and I doubted he was clueless.

"Does that happen often?" I nodded toward the front of the plane where the flight attendant was still eyeing him.

He grimaced. "Way more often than I am comfortable with." His eyes scanned my face. "I'm sure it happens to you as well."

I almost choked on my drink. "Hardly, but I'll take the compliment. Thank you."

"How long has it been since you've seen your family?"

I thought for a second. "My mum and sister came to visit me a year ago, and it was two years before that when I visited, so it's been a while."

He looked into my eyes, and I swear he could see into my soul. He held out his glass to me and said, "Here's to new beginnings for both of us."

I smiled, wondering what my future held. The last thing I wanted was a man in my life, but if I did, he would be a mighty fine candidate.

He must have felt my look because he turned to me with a smile, his eyebrows raised. I cleared my throat and said, "You're right. I shouldn't think of this as the end of something, I should think of this as the beginning."

I motioned to the flight attendant for another drink, but she ignored me, so my seatmate got her attention, ordering another one for both of us. She delivered them right as the plane gave a jolt, and the captain announced over the loudspeaker to put on our seatbelts because of some rough weather ahead. I grabbed each armrest, my hand landing on the arm of my seatmate. I dug my nails in and braced my head against the headrest, closing my eyes tight.

He took my hand in his, wrapping our fingers together. A rush of heat flooded through me, and a soothing voice said, "It's all right. It will be over soon."

I felt like I was on a roller coaster, my stomach rising, heading to my throat with each jerk of the plane.

"What's your name?" he asked.

I tried to swallow, but my mouth was dry. "Molly. Molly McGuire."

"Nice to meet you, Molly McGuire. My name is Liam Fitzgerald."

I lifted my other hand in a half-wave as I focused on my breathing. It felt like forever until the turbulence subsided. After a minute or two, I opened my eyes and cracked my neck to release the tension. I looked for my drink, but it disappeared. I glanced at Liam's tray.

"Didn't want it to spill," he said as he handed me my drink, and I swallowed it in one gulp.

"Whoa, go easy there. That's potent stuff." His head cocked as he looked at me.

"I know." I looked at my hand, still gripping his. I didn't want to let go, but I released my death grip. "I hope I didn't hurt you."

He flexed his fingers and smiled. "I'm fine. I'm more concerned about you. Are you okay?"

I took another deep breath and answered, "Give me a few minutes, and I'll be fine." My head was spinning, and my stomach was doing flip-flops. I wasn't sure if it was from the man next to me or the turbulence.

Dinner came shortly thereafter. Both of us concentrated on our meal. I ate sparingly since my stomach was still feeling wonky, and not long after, the flight attendant collected our trays.

I reclined my seat and closed my eyes. When I woke up, the plane was dark, but I could see bits of sunlight straining to get through the window shades. My watch was still on Michigan time, so I quickly set it ahead by five hours, making it eleven in the morning. I urgently needed to use the toilet but didn't want to wake up Liam. I pushed my footrest down and stood up, grabbing my purse. I turned around, so I was facing him and tried to scoot around his footrest without touching his chair. I was almost out when the person sitting in front of him adjusted his chair, throwing me forward and landed me right in Liam's lap!

My face landed on his chest, and my cheeks burned with embarrassment. The scent of pine and something else tingled my nose. Citrus. Orange? Whatever it was, he smelled superb.

I felt his arms settle around me as he said, "Good morning."

I looked up, and he was grinning. "I am so, so sorry! I was trying to get out, and the chair in front of you moved and—"

"It's all right. I don't mind at all." He was still grinning.

I tried to push myself up, but his arms stopped me. "Um, can you let me go?"

He whispered, "Do I have to?"

My eyes went wide, and he grinned, pushing on the footrest and letting me stand up. Without looking at him, I scurried away and made my way to the toilet at the front of the plane.

Both toilets were occupied, so I had to wait. My body was overheated from what just happened. I wasn't sure if it was his body against mine or just the embarrassment. Either way, I felt like a total idiot.

I could hear dishes clanking from the kitchen area of the plane. The sweet smell of fresh coffee and fresh baked goods tickled my nose and made my stomach growl. How could I possibly be hungry? The toilet finally emptied, so I used the facilities, brushed my teeth, and stopped to look in the mirror. My face was still burning, so I splashed some cold water on it. I added some eyeliner and mascara and looked at my hair. I kept it shoulder length these days, and it didn't look too bad, but I dug out a hairband and placed it on the crown of my head before making my way back to my seat.

Liam was sitting in his chair reading the inflight magazine. I sat down and whispered to him, "I am so sorry for being a klutz. It's an infliction I've had my whole life." I tucked my purse under my seat.

"Not a problem. It's one of my most favorite ways to wake up," he said with a

wink. He leaned into me and whispered. "You're not a klutz; you're gravity challenged."

I laughed. "I'll remember that. My family will love it."

I settled back in my seat, turning on the monitor located in the seat in front of me and checked the flight information. "It looks like we have an hour and forty minutes until we land."

He extended his footrest and said, "In that case, wake me up when the coffee arrives." He closed his eyes, and I could hear his breathing slow as he quickly fell back asleep.

As klutzy as I've been in the past, or "gravity challenged," as he said, falling onto a man's lap was a new one. I grinned at the memory, though. I had to admit it had been nice. A slight beard had appeared on his chin in the past few hours, but the scruffy look only added to the attraction. He had nice lips too, and those eyes! A woman could get lost in those eyes. Oh—and look how long his eyelashes are. Why do men get blessed with those instead of women? It really wasn't fair.

The clanking of the drinks trolly made me avert my gaze before I got caught. Goodness gracious, what am I doing? The last thing I need—or want—is another man in my life!

Most people were awake now, so I lifted the shade from my window, letting the sunshine stream in, but all I could see were clouds, so I pulled it back down.

"Is your family excited you're moving back home?"

"I think so. My younger sister, at least. My parents, of course, and I've really missed my grandparents. My grandmum is eighty-five and going strong. She and I both love mysteries. I used to spend at least one Saturday a month before I moved to America at my grandparents' house watching mystery movies. As a joke last year, Grandmum sent me a lock picking set for Christmas. Can you believe it? I can't wait to show her I actually know how to do it now. I was surprised at how hard it was. They make it look so easy on television."

"A lock picking kit?" He laughed. "That's an original present. Do you have many siblings?"

"There are four of us. I have two older brothers who are twins. Then there is me and my younger sister Fiona. One brother is married with kids. The other will stay an eternal bachelor. How about you?"

"I have a younger sister, married and living in New Zealand. My parents both live in Donegal City, where I'm from, but am currently living in Ballyquicken."

"Wow, New Zealand! How long has it been since you've seen her?"

"I flew there first. I spent ten days with her and then flew to California for a few days."

"You've been away from home quite a while then."

"Yes. It will be good to be home, I miss Sandy." He grinned.

My heart sunk. "Oh, is that your girlfriend?" I swallowed my disappointment.

"Girlfriend?" His eyebrows furrowed, then he smiled. "No, no girlfriend. Man's best friend—Sandy, is my Australian shepherd. She got into some trouble with the neighbor's golden retriever and is due to have puppies next week, and I'm eager to get home to her. A friend of mine is keeping her, but I don't think he and his family will appreciate it if she has her puppies while she's staying there."

My heart lifted. Sandy was his dog! Yippee!

"I love dogs! We had dogs growing up, not that my mum would allow them in the house, and then my husband was allergic, so that didn't work out either. I really miss not having one around."

We chit-chatted until brunch was served. I opted for the spinach quiche and fruit with a side of bacon, and Liam opted for the steak and eggs. We both asked for a second cup of coffee and continued to eat.

"It's nice to see a woman who likes to eat." He took a sip of his coffee.

I lowered my eyes, my cheeks turning red. "I do. My love of food was something my husband got on me about constantly."

"Then good riddance to him. You look great!"

I could feel the heat in my face again, and he grinned.

"I'm sorry. I shouldn't flirt with you like this. It's just been a while since…" His eyes furrowed like he was thinking hard about something.

"Since?"

He averted his eyes back to his meal. I didn't ask again but was very curious about what he was going to say. He lifted a piece of steak to his mouth and then set it back down on his plate. "Since I've met someone I've wanted to flirt with."

Darn this reddish-blond hair. I could feel my face getting warm again. "That's very sweet." I turned my attention to my meal, as did he. I set my fork down and leaned into him.

"I have a confession to make."

He turned his head toward me. "What is it?"

"I don't usually like flirting, but this—it's been nice."

We both smiled and went back to our breakfast.

It wasn't long after when our plane began its descent into Shannon Airport. Before I could grip the armrest, Liam took my hand in his and wound our fingers together. His smooth and calming voice whispering to me. "Just take deep breaths—in slowly and out slowly."

I did my best but couldn't stop the sweat from beading on my forehead. I've never figured out why, but landings always affected me worse than takeoffs. A few minutes later, the plane's wheels hit the ground, and we taxied to the gate.

"Thank you." I looked at him and gave him as much of a smile as I could with my stomach slowly making the trip back down from my throat.

The lights came on, and the click of everyone's seatbelts could be heard throughout the plane. I gathered my things together and waited for the flight attendant to unlock and open the door. As we were in business class, the flight attendants opened the door, and we all stood up. The flight attendants waived us off first, and we made our way down the gangway. Liam and I were side-by-side as we walked into the terminal. I'd had an idea he was tall when he was sitting next to me, but I didn't realize how tall. He was towering over my five-seven.

We were both quiet as we followed the signs to immigration and stood in the queue. The roped line was ten rows deep, and we were about six rows back. Looking at all the people, it reminded me of herded cattle.

"Did you get any sleep?" he asked, setting his carry-on bag on the floor while we waited.

"Some, not a lot. This is the part I hate about flying across time zones, the staying awake as long as you can when you get to your destination to adjust to the new time zone." I pulled out my mobile and turned it on. Once it booted up, I signed onto the airport's Wi-Fi and quickly sent a message to my mum that I'd landed, then stuck the phone back into my purse.

"At least all the booths are open." He nodded toward the front.

I looked toward the front and laughed. "All I see is a sea of people. You have the distinct advantage of being tall."

"It's not always an advantage. When you're trying to blend in, being six-two is definitely a disadvantage." He laughed.

I took off my cardigan sweater and stuffed it into my carry-on as we shuffled our way to the front of the line. Thirty minutes later, it was my turn; a woman motioned me to a booth on the far left. I looked back, noticing Liam headed to the booth on the far right. I handed the lady my Irish passport and immigration slip. After I was through, I followed the signs to the restrooms, then headed to baggage claim.

"Hiya!" Liam had slid up next to me as I walked.

"Hello." I could feel my heart race. What is going on? I cleared my throat and tried to stop myself from doing a little dance right here at baggage claim.

"Do you need a ride?" he asked, then laughed. "I guess I never asked you where you were going, did I?"

I laughed too. "You didn't, but that's all right. I'm going to Dooley. I appreciate the offer, but someone is picking me up. Come to think about it, I'm not sure who. You should know where that is. I forgot. You mentioned you're from Ballyquicken."

"I do, but haven't been there in a while. Nice little village."

"It is. Or at least it was the last time I was here. I'm not sure I'm looking forward to living where everyone knows what's going on in your life. By now I'm sure everyone knows why I've come home." There was that giant squid stuck to my back, waving a giant sign that said "failure."

"It's not a bad thing having such a close community. You know you can always depend on your neighbors to be there for you."

Before I could comment, we heard the clanks and clunks of the luggage belt as it began to turn. A few seconds later, luggage began strewing from the chute and sliding down to the merry-go-round-like monstrosity. A few minutes later, I spotted one of my suitcases and grabbed it off the carousel while searching for my second one. Liam found his, a large black one. He pulled it off the belt and extended the handle. I spotted my second one and ran for it, pulling it off with both hands just before it slipped out of reach. I grunted as I set it on the ground and lifted the handle. Liam came over, and before I could say anything, took the handle and wheeled it toward where the rest of my things were.

"Oh, thank you. You don't have to do that, but I appreciate it. That one is really heavy." I grabbed the rest of my stuff, and we headed toward the area where you can greet your family and friends.

I'd barely walked through the door when I heard a shout, "Molly! Over here! Molly!" I followed the voice, and my heart danced with joy as I spotted Fiona. She was running toward me with her arms extended and almost knocked me down as she enveloped me in an enormous hug.

"You're home. You're home! I can't believe it. I'm so happy." She squeezed me tightly, and I responded in kind, not being able to stop the tears rolling down my face.

I stepped back and looked at her. "You let your hair grow. I like it!" It was almost to her waist, and she was so skinny! She was wearing the cutest flowered dress that showed off her long legs. Her makeup was subtle, and her full lips painted a light rose. After an eight-hour flight, I felt like an ugly duckling.

Fiona looked at Liam and held out her hand. "Hi, I'm Fiona, Molly's sister."

He let go of the suitcase to shake her hand, and it fell to the floor. Both Liam and I bent over at the same time to reach for it and bumped into each other. We came up laughing, both rubbing our heads.

"Sorry," We both said at the same time.

Fiona was grinning. "Still, the klutz, I see."

I looked at Liam and grinned. "I'm not a klutz. I'm gravity challenged."

Liam grinned back, nodding.

"Fiona, this is Liam Fitzgerald. We met on the plane. Liam, my sister Fiona."

Fiona and I are only two years apart, and there were many times as children when that green-eyed monster would come between us. I found it very hard having a gorgeous sister getting all the attention. It happened less and less as we got older, and we're very close now. However, having her meet Liam brought the green-eyed monster back, and I felt like the ugly sister again. She looked as fresh as ever, and I felt like a wet dishrag left in the sink overnight. I looked down at the clothes I'd been wearing for over twenty-four hours and grimaced. My khakis had a stain, my white blouse was wrinkled, and I looked like I'd slept in them. Oh, wait, I had.

Liam shook Fiona's hand. "It's nice to meet you."

We all walked out the door and into the cloudy day, the sun trying to peek through. We stopped when we entered the parking structure. I looked at Liam, trying to memorize every molecule of his gorgeous face. He gazed back, and I could only hope he was doing the same thing. Would I ever see him again?

"I'm headed this way," he pointed toward long term parking. "Fiona, it was nice meeting you, and Molly…it's been a pleasure."

I held out my hand. He clasped it, and my pulse shot to 150. "Thank you very much for helping me get through the flight."

He shot me a salute and walked away. My eyes followed him until I felt a tug on my arm.

"Come on. Everyone is waiting for us at the pub."

"The pub? You're kidding. I have to go take a shower first. I feel gross and grimy.

"You look fine!" She looked at me closer. "Okay, but it has to be a quick one. I will text mom and tell her your flight was late." She pulled out her phone.

I put my hand over hers to stop her. "You can't do that. I already texted her I'd arrived."

"Of course, you did," she rolled her eyes. "When did you text her?"

I could see the sun shining through the door, so I pulled my sunglasses out of my purse and slid them on. "When I was in line at immigration. Why?"

"There we go then. We'll just tell her it took a while to get through."

"Fi, why can't we just tell her we stopped home to take a shower?"

She stopped, her hand on her hip. "Okay fine, but we're stopping at my house. It's closer."

"That's great! I can't wait to see it." I put my arm through hers as we walked outside. "Well, come on then. Let's go. But I'm driving!"

"Oh, no, you're not. American's drive on the wrong side of the road, and you lived there too long."

I elbowed her as I laughed. "Actually, dear sister, American's drive on the right side of the road."

Chapter 2

We walked out to the parking area, and I watched as Fiona hit the button on her key fob, and the lights of an orange, little four-door Mini Cooper lit up. "Nice car! It's a significant improvement over your last one."

Her eyes sparkled. "Is it ever! I just love it—I just bought it last week." She popped the boot, and it was as mini as the rest of the car. I finagled the suitcase and carry-on I'd been holding, but looking at the suitcase she'd been dragging for me, there was no way it would fit, so I closed the boot. I peeked into the rear window at the back seat and then looked at her.

"It will fit." She opened up the rear door and pulled the driver seat forward. It took both hands for her to lift it up, but it was too big to slide in.

I walked to the passenger side door and opened it, ducking in. "Here, let me pull while you push."

It took some maneuvering, but we got it in. I just wasn't sure if we'd ever get it out again.

"Did you have to bring the largest suitcase on the market?" she asked as we both got in the car, and she started it up.

"It's hard to go through five years of your life and decide what to throw away and what to keep. They only allowed me two free bags. Wait until you see all the boxes I had shipped." I moved my bottom around on the seat. "This is nice, Fi. I love the leather seats. Oh, and navigation too? You went for all the bells and whistles," I attached my seatbelt and settled my purse at my feet.

"Yes, navigation was a must. You know I have no sense of direction."

I smiled at the comment. She couldn't read a map to save her life. GPS was made for someone like her.

We headed south out of Shannon on the N-18, cars and lorry's whizzing by until we got out of the city. The rolling, green hills greeted us as we merged onto N-69 toward the coast. The land looked like a patchwork quilt in multiple shades of green, fences built of stone marking the neighbors' boundaries. Once we came to the city of Foynes, we traveled the coast of the River Shannon until we came to Tarbert, then inland again.

I turned towards Fi. "I missed this! Everything is so green and vast. I'd forgotten just how beautiful it is." The rolling green hills with sheep dotted throughout made me smile. "Do the parents still have sheep?"

"A few. They're concentrating more on the beef side of things, but they sell some wool to the locals. The problem is sheep like to roam."

"Better a roaming sheep than a roaming husband," I murmured.

"I'm sorry things didn't work out with Keith." She laid her hand over mine.

My gaze left the scenery to look at her. "Thanks, sis. I knew things weren't working. It just took me a while to do something about it." I looked out the window again, not seeing the beautiful scenery, but the past five years flicker by like a silent movie. My mind went back to the last fight we'd had, which ended with Keith asking for a divorce and moving out. I took a deep breath. "Moving back here was the right decision. I don't know what my future holds, but I have faith everything will work out." I'd spent too much time wondering what went wrong with my marriage. I was here to start over, putting the past behind me.

"How are the grandparents?"

"Gram is doing great, but Gramps is slowing down. I think the parents are going to ask them to move into the manor."

We'd lost my dad's parents several years ago in an auto accident, which hit the family hard. Having my mum's parents around definitely helped us all heal. They stepped in and kept us all busy. My grandmum kept us girls busy watching old black and white movies, and Grandpa spent time with the boys, fishing and hiking.

I looked at her then. "That would be great! But I can't see them agreeing. They like their independence too much."

"Plus, Gram and our mum are too much alike. They'd end up killing each other." We both chuckled.

"Have you seen Mrs. Riley lately?" Her image popped into my head. Not much over five feet tall with dark auburn hair, she would wear up in a bun, running around in jeans and a sweatshirt with the store's logo on it. The widowed bookstore owner was one of my favorite people. I worked for her and her husband all through school. I'd already had a love of books, but working there was quite the education.

"I ran into her the other day. She was very excited to hear you're back. She wants you to come and see her as soon as you can."

"I will. I've missed her. We kept in touch when I first left, but our communication dwindled as time went by. Some of my best childhood memories are of that bookstore. First, Mum taking us in to buy books, then my working there. It seems so long ago."

As we drove along, the clouds became thicker and turned from a light gray to an angry gray, and soon, the drops started to fall. There was a boom of thunder, and the rain came splashing down like someone had opened up a dam in the heavens.

Fi turned on her windshield wipers, and I couldn't help but open the window and breathe it all in.

"Hey, close the window! You'll get soaked."

"You don't understand! Nothing smells as sweet as a good ole' Irish thunderstorm." I stuck my head out further, letting the rain hit my face.

She laughed. "You are crazy! Were you always like this or did your time in America do this to you?"

I closed the window. "I realized on the plane ride over here how I need to see all of this as the beginning of something, not the end. Maybe it brought out the little kid in me again."

Ten minutes later, the rain stopped, and the sun broke out from under the clouds. I was scanning the sky when I spotted it. "Fiona, look!" I said as I pointed to the right. "Isn't it beautiful!" The rainbows seemed to stretch across the sky; the vibrant colors made me feel like I could reach out and grab it.

I looked at Fiona, and she was grinning. I laughed. "I know, I'm crazy." I looked out the window again but kept on talking. "How's your job going?"

"It's great. My boss is pretty nice. I didn't think I'd like being a web designer, but it seems everyone wants a website these days, so I'm very busy."

"That's good. I have no idea what I'm going to do. Thankfully, I have enough money to last me a while until I decide."

Fiona started talking, and I tuned her out, thinking about my past, present, and future. I laid my head back on the headrest and closed my eyes.

I felt a slap on my arm. "So, do you?"

It pulled me out of my reverie. "Ow! Do I what?"

"Do you think Liam might get in touch with you? If he does, you could ask him to the gala."

"What gala?" I asked, rubbing my arm.

"Didn't Mum tell you? The town is having a festival this Friday and Saturday to help raise funds for the church roof. It all ends Saturday night with a special gala the parents are hosting at the manor. It's all very formal."

"You're kidding?" I thought back to what I'd packed. "I'm sure I have nothing to wear. I can't believe she didn't mention it."

"You know what this means?" She grinned.

"Yes, that I will be totally embarrassed showing up in my nightgown and slippers, which is the closest thing I have to an evening gown."

"Oh, I would love to see Mum's face if you were to do that, but no, I meant we need to go shopping. We have a great little boutique in town that you will love! We must go there soon. But what about Liam? Are you going to ask him to the dance?"

I turned to look at her. "Really, Fi. We only just met and flirted a little, but that's all. I'll probably never see him again." My stomach sank at the thought.

"There's always Callum. He's still available."

Memories of my childhood friend made me smile. There were four of us who hung out together. Callum, myself, Reanna, and my now sister-in-law, Ciara. We used to get into so much trouble. Then, as we got older, Ciara started dating my brother Aiden, Reanna was busy with her own life, which left Callum and me to grow closer—until that fateful trip to Michigan when I met Keith.

"I thought he and Margery O'Connor got married not long after I left."

"They did. Then, a few years later, they divorced. You broke his heart when you left, and dear old Margery was there to pick up the pieces."

"I'm sure she did." If anyone were to ask me if there was anyone on this earth I truly hated, it would be Margery. Every school has its mean girls, and Margery was the leader of the pack. I ignored her as much as possible, but throughout the years, we crossed paths, such as being forced by my parents to attend her birthday parties. My guess is because she didn't have any friends. As we got older, every time a boy seemed to be interested in me, she would do her best to steal his attention. She also almost got me expelled when she stole Mary Dugan's bracelet and planted it in my backpack.

"Well, she's a widow now. She married some old guy in Cork who died under mysterious circumstances and left her a colossal amount of money. I'm not sure why she moved back to Dooley. She didn't say anything but kept glancing at me.

"What?" I asked.

"I didn't want to be the one to tell you this, but it's probably better you're prepared."

"Prepared for what?" I asked, fiddling with the necklace I was wearing.

"For the news that Dillon is dating Margery."

"Our Dillon? As in our older brother?" I stared at her. "You're joking, right?"

"Yes, our brother. No, I'm not joking," she croaked out.

"What on earth would make that man want to date her?" I thought about her reputation when we were in school. "Never mind. I know why."

I sat back in my seat, trying to get the image of the two of them out of my head when a thought struck, "Please tell me he's not thinking of marrying her?" I was sure my head would explode if that happened.

"I don't think so, but I've only seen them together a few times at the bar. It's not like he's brought her to any of the family gatherings or anything." Fiona turned on the rural road headed for Dooley. I'd forgotten how narrow the roads are here. Which reminded me how I'll need to get a vehicle. I brought out my phone and started to make a list of all the things I needed to do.

"So why an orange car?" To the list, I added car, change phone company, find a cottage, a job, and change bank as she answered.

She laughed. "If you remember, my old car was blue. It always seemed when I was looking for it in a crowded parking lot, there were always a bunch of blue cars. I figured purchasing an orange car would stand out, and it does."

Fiona's home was a delightful, three-bedroom, whitewashed cottage that looked like something out of a tourist book or website on visiting Ireland. I didn't have time to take in all the details, as Mum had already texted me asking where we were. I took the quickest shower ever, dried my hair, and we were on our way to the pub within thirty minutes.

Chapter 3

I'd changed from my filthy airplane clothes to the two least wrinkled items in my suitcase. I hope no one expected me to walk in looking like a fashion model, not that I could anyway, but I had found a denim skirt that ended right above my knees, and a green and white long-sleeved Michigan State University Spartan tee-shirt with the University's mascot, "Sparty" on the front.

Fi's cottage was only two blocks from the pub, so it didn't take long for us to get there. Fi stopped at a stop sign, and I was able to look down High Street at all the multi-colored shops lining the road down to the sea. I opened the window again and took a deep breath.

"I have missed the smell of the sea!"

A beep from the car behind us got Fiona going again. She pressed on the gas, and a block later, we arrived.

Our twin brothers, Aiden and Dillon, owned Shenanigans, the one and only pub in town. I couldn't believe our luck when a car pulled out of the space right in front. Fiona pulled her compact car in and turned off the engine. I practically jumped out of the car.

The building was an extensive stone structure that dated back to the 1700s. I pushed open the heavy oak door to the sound of laughter and clinking glasses. Then, the scent of stale beer hit me as we walked farther into the room. A fire was blazing in the stone fireplace on the wall to our left, burning out the chill of the cool June day. I looked around, taking it all in. The dark, oak bar sat against the wall to the right, the restrooms located down the hall beyond. The back wall sported an enormous Irish flag, it's orange, white and green stripes showing our Irish pride. The kitchen was located behind that wall. The doors swung wildly as the staff brought food out to all of the hungry patrons. My uncle had owned the bar until five years ago when he died in a car accident. My siblings and I spent many a night at this pub playing with my cousins, enjoying a good craic. Both my brothers had worked here from the time they were old enough and were very close to Uncle Sean. As a childless bachelor, he left his prize possession to them.

We walked deeper into the bar, and I said, "It's packed!"

Fiona shrugged. "I guess the word is out you're back."

Ha! Any reason to take the afternoon off and go to the pub was more like it. I glanced around the room, looking for people I recognized. I waved to my aunt and uncle and noticed some friends of my parents and more than a few cousins. Even Dad Kearney was here. My eyes lit up when they fell on the group sitting at a long table in the middle of the room. My dad looked a little grayer, and my mum showing a wrinkle or two more than a year ago, but I was ecstatic to see them. Mum was smiling, one of Aiden's twins standing close to her, her arm around him. Evan or Ethan? It will probably take me a while to tell the twins apart. There were a few empty chairs next to my parents with coloring books and crayons, so I assumed those were where the kids were sitting, and she hadn't brought those for me. However, I do enjoy a good coloring session.

Across from them were my brother, Aiden, and his wife, Ciara, with two seats empty next to them.

We walked up to the table, and Fiona announced, "Here she is!"

The crowd went silent until my mum shrieked, "Fiona Marie, you were supposed to let me know when you left the airport!" She stood up so quickly her chair would have fallen had my dad not caught it in time. She ran to me. I fell into her arms.

The crowd started talking again, and I heard several people shout, "Welcome back," and other niceties, but I held my mum tightly and couldn't stop the tears from falling down my face.

"Oh, darling, it's so nice to have you back where you belong." She squeezed me tighter.

I stepped back, and Dad, who had snuck up behind her, pulled me into his arms. "Kitten, it's so good to see you."

The tears fell harder as they passed me from person to person, ending with one of my best friends and sister-in-law, Ciara.

We hugged each other tightly as I said, "I have missed you so much!"

Once the hug ended, she said, "I've missed you too. I'm so glad you're back. Reanna wanted me to tell you she couldn't get the afternoon off, but to call her when you get settled in. Otherwise, she'll see you Saturday night at the gala."

I'd known Ciara since we were six years old. Her mum was one of my mum's oldest friends, so we'd gotten together a lot when we were young. We met Reanna when we were ten, and she was like another sister to us. We played together, went to school together, went through puberty together, and got in trouble together. Callum joined the group when we were twelve, and as much as our parents hoped he'd be able to keep us out of trouble, he joined in.

The tears kept coming, and someone stuck a tissue in my hand, so I blew my nose and stuck it in my pocket. I waved to my aunt and uncle and all the cousins who were there and sat down at the table.

"Where are the rest of the kids?" I asked, looking around. The twin near my mum had disappeared, and I didn't see his look-alike, or their youngest, Kaleigh.

Aiden answered, "Probably getting into trouble." He smiled, which quickly turned into a frown as he scanned the room.

My dad smiled and said, "It's called karma."

My mum sat next to me, so Fiona took the chair she had vacated.

Mum added, "That's for sure. You have what's coming to you, Aiden Patrick. You and Dillon scared me to death with your shenanigans when you were kids."

"Mum, we had a nanny! And she didn't tell you half of the stuff we did," Dillon added, looking at Aiden, a grin on his face.

"I knew more than you think I did, young man. Miss Parkins reported to me every night after you were both in bed. Do you know how many times we had to raise her pay so she wouldn't quit? You ran her ragged!"

I smiled as I watched my family interact. How I missed them! Aiden and Dillon were identical twins, a little easier to tell apart now, as Aiden had a face full of hair, and Dillon preferred a smooth shave. They loved to trade places with each other when they were younger, causing all kinds of mischief.

Aiden added, "We treated Nanny Parkins badly. She used to tell us she never worried about us when we argued. It was when we got along that we were our most mischievous." Everyone laughed.

A little girl with red hair and freckles ran up to the table and into Aiden's arms. She was as cute as a button, dressed in a flowery dress with little white socks and black patent-leather shoes. I couldn't help but notice the lace on the front of her dress was torn, and she had a line of dirt on her face. She was a kid after my own heart. She leaned up to whisper in her dad's ear. Aiden's smile widened as he nodded toward me and said, "Yes, this is your Aunt Molly."

She gave me a wide-eyed look. "Did you really come from America?"

I leaned in closer to her so she could hear me over the crowd. "I did! On a huge airplane."

"Are you really, my aunt? Like Aunt Fiona?" She leaned over the table toward me.

"I am. Are you really Kaleigh? My niece?" I asked, biting back a smile as she looked serious with her finger against her cheek, her elbow on the table.

She giggled, sitting back in her dad's lap. "Yes. I am Kaleigh Lynn Quinn, and I am four years old. How old are you?"

The entire family laughed at that question. "Come here, and I'll tell you," I said, crooking my finger at her.

She crawled down from her dad's lap and came over to me. I pushed out my chair and pulled her on to my lap.

"So, you want to know how old I am?" I had to bite my lip to not laugh.

"Yep."

I smiled at her as I put my hand on her stomach and tickled her. "Not as old as your daddy!"

We both started giggling, and her feet rose, kicking Mum's arm.

"Okay, you two, settle down," My mum said, scowling.

Kaleigh and I looked at each other and at the same time, said, "Sorry."

Kaleigh looked at me, wrapped her arms around my neck, and whispered into my ear, "I think I'm going to like you."

I smiled and whispered back, "I think I'm going to like you too." I gave her an enormous hug.

"Kaleigh, come here for a minute," said Ciara. She hopped off my lap and walked over to her mum. "What happened here?" she asked, pointing at the torn lace.

Kaleigh looked down at her dress, and then looked at her mom and tilting her head, "Mama, I told you I should have worn pants and a tee-shirt, but you wouldn't listen."

Ciara laughed and said, "You said that, didn't you?" She picked up a napkin, dipped it in her glass of water, and cleaned the dirt off Kaleigh's face. "What were you and your brothers up to that you're so dirty?"

Instead of answering, she kissed her mum on the cheek and hopped off her lap.

"Just once I'd like to get that child in a dress and her act like a little girl," Ciara said, frowning. "Aiden—"

"On my way." Aiden got up and went to find out what his offspring were up to.

"She is so cute. Give her a break, though. I was just like that when I was her age. I had two twin brothers just like her. I wanted to do everything they did, and I couldn't do it in a dress."

"Deidre, was Molly hard to get into a dress when she was Kaleigh's age?" Ciara asked Mum.

She nodded. "Impossible, except on Sundays, and that's because she knew she didn't have a choice."

I moved the menu to cover my face and part of Ciara's as I whispered, "And I changed my clothes as soon as we returned home from church so I could play tag with the boys."

I had just taken a sip of my beer when Dillon popped up from the table and said, "I'll be right back."

I turned and watched as he met a woman on her way to our table, took her arm, and tried to turn her back toward the door.

"Is that who I think it is?" I didn't really expect an answer because she had changed little in the time I'd been away. It was Margery O'Connor—or whatever her current last name was.

She practically pulled Dillon back to the table, and when that didn't work, she dislodged her arm from his and walked toward our table. She was dressed in a short red dress with a jean jacket over it, and tall, black heels tapping on the floor as she walked. Her long black hair had some curl to it, and I could see the long black earrings swinging as she stood at the end of the table.

She said loudly, "I just want to welcome your darling sister back from the States, Dillon."

I stopped myself from telling her she was the last person I wanted to see—ever. I didn't want to make a scene.

"What are you doing here, Margery?" I clenched my hands together as a reminder to be nice.

"I know we weren't very close at school, but I hope we can be friends now that Dillon and I are a couple."

"Um…okay. I look forward to it." I didn't, really.

"Shall we do lunch soon?" She smiled, but it didn't quite make it to her eyes.

"Oh, let's do. Have your assistant call my assistant and set it up." I smiled politely.

"I don't have an assistant. Do you have an assistant?" She ran her hands through her hair. "Dillon, why would she have an assistant?"

Before I could answer, Dillon took her by the arm and turned her around. "This isn't the best time, Margery. Why don't I show you out?"

I watched Dillon lead her to the door, wondering what he sees in her. She is one of those people God puts on earth to test whether the rest of us have the self-discipline not to kill them. I picked up my purse and said to the table, "I'm headed to the bar. Does anyone want anything?"

Everyone started shouting out orders. I had to take a pen and notebook out of my purse to write them all down. I headed to the bar where Dillon was standing, talking to the bartender. He looked at me when I laid my hand on his shoulder.

"Sorry about that, sis. I asked her not to show up today. I wanted to let you know first we were dating."

"Fiona broke the news on the ride from the airport. I thought you had enough sense not to get involved with her."

"Yeah, I've been trying to break up with for a week, but she refuses to accept it. What was I thinking?" He looked at the bartender and said, "Scott, I'll take another beer, please." He sat down on the stool standing between us, rubbing his hand over his face.

I bumped him with my shoulder. "You've never had the best choice in women."

He bumped back. "I know."

Scott handed him a beer, and Dillon said to him, "Scott, I'd like you to meet my little sister, Molly, fresh off the boat from America."

I looked at Dillon and then at Scott, holding out my hand. "It was a plane, actually, but it's nice to meet you."

"Boat, plane, whatever," Dillon said as he took a long draw of his beer.

Scott shook my hand and said, "It's nice to meet you. Did you just get in?"

I nodded, "Just a couple of hours ago."

"What can I get you then? I'm sure Dillon won't mind if it's on the house." He gave my brother a smile.

"Go ahead. It's fine by me," he said as he took another sip of beer.

"You're going to think this is crazy, but I have been craving a Guinness ever since I knew I was coming home."

Scott drew back the tap, "They have Guinness in America, don't they?"

I nodded. "They do, but it's not as good, and they don't know how to pour it. Or it doesn't taste as good because they don't know how to pour it. I'm not sure which."

He held the glass at a forty-five-degree angle and let the beer pour into the glass, slowly leveling the glass as it filled. He sat the glass in front of me, and I watched the brew settle, the distinct shades of brown coming together, the foam reaching almost to the top. Scott set it down to settle, and a few seconds later, topped it off and set it in front of me.

"I can't believe I'm so excited to drink a beer!" I said as I lifted it up and took a drink, letting the perfect balance of sweet and bitter roll around on my tongue and to the back of my throat.

"It's perfect!" I said. "Thank you!"

"Anytime. Do you need anything else?" he asked, taking a rag and cleaning the counter.

"Oh, goodness, yes. I have a bunch of orders for you from our table." I started rattling them off, and Dillon moved from his seat and went around the bar.

"I'll get these. Scott, help Lucy," he said as he nodded to the server waiting at the other end of the bar.

Dillon started making the drinks, and I said, "Oh, I'd like some fish and chips, please."

Dillon put the order in and then grabbed a tray, adding our drinks one by one, scowling the whole time.

"You okay big brother?" I asked as I took another sip of my beer.

"Just grand," he said, picking up the tray.

"I can take that."

He laughed and said, "No way am I letting my klutzy sister take five drinks to a table halfway across the pub."

I pushed away from the bar and walked behind him, "I'm not a klutz! I am gravity challenged!"

We all sat down again, but Dillon was quiet as everyone else chatted and laughed. My fish and chips came, and I have to say, no one makes chips like the Irish. They were thick, the outside crispy, and the inside done perfectly. They were yummy.

Time flew by as we chatted. Many people dropped by to say hello and to welcome me back. Not long after, exhaustion caught up with me, and I had to hide a yawn behind my hand as I glanced at my watch. It was after eight. I looked at Fiona and asked, "Are you ready to go?"

She was reading a text, and then her thumbs started flying. "I have a date."

Mum heard the word "date" and sat up straighter. "Did you just make this date? That's not very gentlemanly."

She rolled her eyes. "We had tentative plans; he wasn't sure if he'd get out of work in time. We're just going to the café for a snack. Can you drive Molly to your house?"

"I suppose so." She looked at Dad, "Joseph, are you ready to go?"

He'd been talking to one of his friends, who said goodbye, and looked at his wife." Did I hear something about taking Molly home?"

Chapter 4

After saying thank you and goodbye to everyone, I walked out, my parents and Fiona following. She popped the boot of her car, and I grabbed my belongings.

"Is that all you brought?" My mum asked.

Fiona piped in, "No, the largest and most cumbersome suitcase is back here," she pointed to the suitcase wedged in her backseat.

The parents walked over, and my mum laughed. "I don't suppose this is a convertible?"

"No, unfortunately," Fiona replied.

Dad raised his eyebrows, a grin on his face. "Do you want it to be?"

Her eyes opened wide, "Only if you want to buy me a new one."

Being awake for over thirty hours was taking its toll, so I opened up the back-passenger door and said, "Fiona, open the door. We will just do this in reverse of how we got it in. I push, you pull."

Fiona opened the door, and I counted, "One–two–three, and I pushed."

"Ow!" Fiona yelled.

"What happened?" I asked, popping my head out of the backseat.

"You smacked it right into my nose!" She touched her hand to it and yelled, "It's bleeding!" She looked at me and said, "You gave me a bloody nose!"

Mum ran to her. "Tip your head back, honey. We'll go back into the bar and get a cold cloth." She gave me an evil look as she opened the door for Fiona.

I turned toward Dad. "I didn't do it on purpose!"

He laughed. "You still have the magic touch, don't you?"

I groaned. "I thought you said I'd outgrow it when I grew up."

He chuckled again. "Obviously, that hasn't happened yet." He winked at me. "Come on, let's get this suitcase out of here, and I'll take you home." He walked over to where I was standing and said, "But this time, I'll push, you pull."

After we finagled the suitcase out of Fiona's backseat and into my parents' Land Rover, the sun was going down, and more clouds were moving in. "I'd better go see how Fiona's doing. Are you coming with me?"

I shook my head. "I think I'll walk home if that's okay. I need to wake up."

"Are you sure?"

I nodded. "The walk will do me good."

"Okay, but Mol?"

I looked at him, and he said, "Be careful. It's not the village you left five years ago." He turned and walked into the pub.

I started walking down the road, wondering what he meant, when I heard a car pull up behind me. My dad's warning rang in my head, and I looked around to see where I could run.

"Hey, you eejit, get out of the road!"

I turned around to give the driver a piece of my mind when I noticed it was a Garda car, known in the United States as a police car. A man was hanging out of the driver's window, his brown hair blowing in the wind with a sappy grin on his face.

"Callum, is that you?"

His grin widened as he jumped out of the car, closed his door, but left the engine running.

"You big goof! You scared me to death!" I said as he walked toward me. His arms reached out, and he grabbed me by the waist and twirled me around.

"Stop it! I hate when you do this!"

He put me down and said, "No, you don't."

I grinned, "You're right. I don't. How have you been?" He looked good. The blue uniform looked good on him.

He gave me a big hug and said, "Good. I heard you were coming home. When did you get in?

"A few hours ago. Fiona was supposed to drive me, but she asked our parents to do it. Then, I gave Fiona a bloody nose, which delayed my parents, and I was ready to go home, so here I am!"

"Still a klutz?" He laughed.

I punched him in the arm, "I'm not a klutz!" I thought of Liam as I added, "I am gravity challenged." Maybe if I said it enough, people would believe it. I looked at his car. "Mind giving me a ride?"

He looked at the car and then at me and said, "Well, it's against regulations, but why not? Hop in."

I got in the passenger door and sat down. "Will you get in trouble?"

He laughed. "Probably, but when has that stopped us?"

"So true. However, if I remember correctly, the last time we got in trouble, it was Ciara's fault. Remember? We'd gone on a bike ride, and she was hungry and wanted to steal an apple from the Sullivans' farm. We got in so much trouble."

He nodded. "My parents grounded me for two weeks! Those were the days, weren't they?"

"They were! So, what made you become a police officer?" I asked. "I know, it was this or jail, right?"

He grinned. "Hilarious. I've always wanted to be one just like my Uncle Patrick. It took me a few years to make the decision, but I applied, and here I am."

"Oh, my goodness, I remember him. He was a really big guy, right? Bald? He used to scare the heck out of me."

"That was him. He scared a lot of my friends. I think he did it on purpose, but I loved it when he came over and told stories of taking down evil guys."

"I'm sorry things didn't work out with Margery."

His smile faded as he nodded. "It wasn't the best idea I've ever had, but by the time I realized it, it was too late. It was a long time ago, and we've both moved on."

"Did you know she's dating Dillon?"

He nodded. "I'd heard a rumor. I just figured he was smarter than that."

"Me too. She came in the bar tonight, and Dillon asked her to leave. She didn't look very pleased."

"She's never pleased these days. I try to stay away from her. I am so glad you're back, even if it isn't under the best of circumstances."

"Good to know the village grapevine is still up and running. Yes, Keith and I are in the process of a divorce, and since I had nothing keeping me in the States, I moved back here."

I looked out the window as we came to a white split-rail fence that marked the border between our house and the Kellys' property next to us. I smiled as Callum turned into the estate entrance, the tree-lined driveway feeling like we'd entered a forest. As Callum drove, my excitement at being home grew. The immense structure was originally built in the late 1600s and totally refurbished in the early 1800s in the Victorian style. Built of mostly brick, the enormous house had four floors, the ground floor holding a ballroom. My great-granddad, granddad, and now my dad, have lived here their entire lives, and I'm sure my dad will die here. The family money ran out a long time ago, but some solid investments and my dad being a lawyer—sorry, solicitor, is what keeps the place from falling down. It was previously a potato farm, but over the past fifty years, the family expanded into sheep, and now cattle.

And it was home. Callum pulled into the circle drive, and I was practically bouncing in my seat.

There was an enormous grin on his face as he looked at me. "You're still just a goofy kid, aren't you?"

I had to laugh. "I've spent the past five years trying to hide my Irish roots because Keith didn't approve. I know it sounds silly, but I feel like I'm finally beginning to feel like…well, feel like me again."

"That doesn't sound silly. I don't think I could hide who I am, and I'm sorry you had to."

"Thanks. Would you like to come in for some coffee?"

"I'd better not. I'm on duty and am supposed to be out on patrol. Do you have a date for the gala yet?"

I laughed. "I just found out about it a few hours ago. Not only do I not have a date; I don't have a dress."

"Well, if you find a dress, will you go with me?" He smiled, and I looked at those big brown eyes.

I smiled at him and said, "It's a date."

I got out of the car, and he waited until I was at the door before he drove away. I turned the handle, and it didn't open, so I used the knocker, expecting Higgins, the butler, to open it. Since there was no answer, I went around to the back and in through the kitchen.

Mrs. Jones, the live-in cook and housekeeper, was cleaning the counters as I walked in. I snuck up behind her and said, "How is my favorite housekeeper?"

The small, rotund lady with gray hair jumped three feet as she turned around. "You about scared five years off of me, Miss Molly, and I don't have too many to spare!"

I gave her a huge hug. "How have you been?" She had bags under her eyes and a few more wrinkles, but she was as spry as ever.

"My rheumatism is acting up now and again, but that doesn't stop me."

Just then, the teapot whistled. "Would you like a cup of tea, darlin'?"

"Mrs. Jones, I would love one. No one in America knows how to make a decent cup of tea."

She laughed as she added the tea to the pot and then the boiling water. She tried to stop me, but I got the rest of the items together and placed them all on the tray. Before she could, I grabbed the tray and set it on the table, and we both sat down. I went to pour it, but she slapped my hand.

"I expected Higgins to answer the door, where is he?"

"It's his day off. Now, tell me all about America," she said as she poured the tea.

I woke up the next morning to someone knocking on the bedroom door. I lifted my head off the pillow and yelled, "Come in," and laid it back down. The door opened with my mum carrying a tray.

I sat up and asked, "What's this? Breakfast in bed?" She looked lovely as always, dressed in a pair of white linen slacks and a yellow short-sleeved blouse. Even without makeup, she looked incredible.

"Don't get used to it, but Mrs. Jones made you a full Irish breakfast, and I didn't have the heart to tell her you weren't awake yet."

"What time is it?" I asked as she set the tray on my lap and poured me a cup of tea before sitting down on the end of the bed.

"A little after eight. How did you sleep?"

"Good. Sorry I wasn't awake when you and Dad returned home. How is Fiona?" I asked, taking a sip of tea. I set it down and added two teaspoons of sugar, ignoring the frown that appeared on her face.

"She'll be fine. We ended up calling the doctor to make sure it wasn't broken. She's wearing a hideous bandage over her nose. You should be more careful, dear."

I set my tea down with a clatter. "I didn't do it on purpose! It was an accident." I picked up my fork and stabbed at my eggs.

"I know it was, but you know how—"

"I'm not klutzy, Mum. I'm gravity challenged."

She smiled. "Whatever you call it, you just need to be more careful."

I stayed quiet, stabbing my eggs.

"What are you going to do today?" she asked as she lifted herself off the bed.

I swallowed my eggs and picked up my tea. I looked around the room. My two suitcases had appeared overnight, sitting next to the vanity. "I guess the first thing is unpack and then try to get a date for when the rest of my stuff will arrive."

"Stuff, dear? You really spent too much time in America."

I stopped myself from rolling my eyes. I should have moved in with Fiona.

"Stuff as in things. When my personal items will arrive."

"Now you're just being smart." She opened the door, stopping to ask, "Do you require any help with your unpacking?"

I finished my cup of tea and poured another one, again adding two teaspoons of sugar.

"Dear, you really should watch your sugar intake. It's not very good for you."

"I know." I took a deep breath. "Aren't you busy with the gala?"

"Yes, but I could help you if you need it."

"I think I can handle it. I hope you don't mind that I took this room."

"Of course not. It was your room growing up. We will have a full house this weekend, though, just fair warning."

"I figured. How many are attending?"

"We have a little over two hundred right now. I'm not sure if they'll all fit in the ballroom. I have extra help arriving soon to help Mrs. Jones with the cleaning, so you might see strangers walking around."

"Thanks for the warning." I smiled.

I looked down at the food still left on my plate, realizing there was no way I could eat it all. I ate what I could and then took a shower. This bedroom shared a bathroom with the room next door, which used to be Fiona's room. I pulled out a pair of jeans and a sweatshirt and dragged the largest suitcase onto the bed.

Although this was my room when I lived here years ago, it had been redecorated and painted in a lovely shade of lilac with white trim. I had to admit it looked nice with the slightly darker purple carpet. The bedframe was white, the sheets and comforter a lovely shade of lilac with purple and pink flowers throughout. The vanity and the two dressers were also white, with the dresser drawers painted the same color as the room.

I pulled clothes out of the suitcase and laid them on the bed. It had been warm when I left the U.S., and I realized as I unpacked both suitcases, I hadn't exactly packed for a June in Ireland, which is more like a March in Michigan. Other than a few sweaters and jeans, I sent all of my fall and winter clothes via post. What was I thinking?

I put away the clothes appropriate for the weather in the one dresser, leaving the clothes I wouldn't wear for months, if at all, into the large suitcase. I stuck both suitcases in the closet and dug my laptop out of my carry-on to check my email. Before I knew it, a loud, vibrating sound reached me, and my heart practically jumped out of my chest. It took a minute to realize it was the lunch gong.

I washed up in the bathroom and headed downstairs, pleasantly surprised to see my dad sitting at the table. I kissed his cheek.

"What are you doing home?" I asked as I sat down at the table, placing my napkin on my lap.

"I thought I would come and see my lovely daughter. What have you been doing this morning?"

Mrs. Jones brought in the soup and filled our bowls. It felt so surreal to have someone waiting on me. In my old life, lunch was usually a quick salad I'd taken with me to work.

"Nothing much. I spent most of the morning unpacking and trying to track down when my things will be here."

"Were you able to find out?" Dad asked, dipping into his soup.

"Yes. They should be here by the end of the week."

Mum's head popped up. "The end of the week? We have guests coming on Friday."

How many boxes are we talking? We can't have boxes around everywhere."

Before I could answer, Dad said, "Deidre, calm down. I'm sure we can put them in the spare garage for now." He winked at me before going back to his soup.

I smiled. "Thank you, Dad. I can't believe Stewart is still here." He seemed old when I was a child. Now he must be ancient.

He nodded. "The delivery driver will most likely take that number of packages to the garage anyway, but I'll let Stewart know they'll be coming."

I took a sip of water. "Fi mentioned you got rid of most of the sheep and are concentrating on cattle?"

"Yes. I'm taking this afternoon off. A calf is sick."

"Oh, so it wasn't me you came home to see." I grinned.

He laughed. "Well, let's just say it was a bonus."

The next course comprised roast beef and potatoes, and Dad was very proud to say it was from one of our stock. He spent the next thirty minutes explaining to me why he was switching from sheep to cattle. Basically, it's a money thing.

I looked at both of my parents, "I need to get a vehicle. Any idea where I should start looking?" I asked.

Mum laughed. "Fi bought hers over the Internet. Can you believe it?"

"Really? Without even a test drive?" That didn't sound like her.

"I guess she found it on some website and then checked it out. I think she ended up buying it in Ballyquicken, didn't she, Joseph?"

"Yes, I believe so," he answered. He looked at me and asked, "How are you set for money, Molly? Do you need a loan?" He sat back in his chair as Mrs. J came and cleared his plate.

"Thanks, Dad, but I'm set pretty well for now, and when the house sells, I'll be even better."

"Have there been any offers?" Mum asked.

"I received an email this morning with a substantial offer. As long as Keith doesn't have any issues with it, hopefully, it will be sold soon."

"That's great, honey," Dad said. "You can use my car this afternoon if you'd like."

"I'd like to stop by and see the grandparents, so that would be great, thanks."

"Oh, that reminds me, honey, I've invited them for dinner this evening, so if there are other things you need to do, they'll be here around six."

"Fiona mentioned you're trying to convince them to move in here. I think that's a great idea."

Mum looked at Dad. "It was your dad's idea, actually. However, I have to admit they're getting older and I worry about them on their own."

Dad chuckled. "What she's not saying is she's afraid she and Bridget won't be able to live together after all these years."

"I can relate." I grinned at Mum. Her mouth fell open, and then she too grinned.

"We can bring it up again tonight, but they're pretty stubborn." Mum rose from the table as one of the maids came and started clearing it off.

"I'll be in my sitting room if anyone needs me. I have details to confirm for the gala." Mum gave Dad a kiss on the cheek and disappeared.

Chapter 5

After lunch, I went back upstairs and looked for something more suitable to wear. After a quick search, I decided on a pair of jeans, along with a white blouse that wasn't too wrinkled and then threw a light-blue crewneck sweater over it. I pulled my tall brown boots out of the closet, tucking my jeans into them, grabbed my coat, and purse and was back downstairs in time to catch Dad before he headed outside.

He showed me where he kept his keys, and I headed outside. I went to get into the car on the left side, realizing the steering wheel is on the right side. This made me hesitate for an instant, making a mental note to drive on the left side of the road and not the right. My drive into town was slow and steady.

Since I would see my grandparents that evening, my first stop was on High Street at the mobile phone store to switch from my U.S. phone plan to a local one. It took a lot longer than I'd hoped, and as I walked out two hours later, I realized the bakery Reanna owned was right across the street and headed that way.

A wave of cinnamon and chocolate greeted me as I walked in, making my mouth water. My eyes found the displays of cakes, cookies, cupcakes, and pie like a magnet. There were so many choices; I blocked out my other senses until I heard a familiar voice.

"May I help you?"

I lifted my head and grinned. "Surprise!"

"Molly?" Her eyes went wide as she came out from behind the counter. "I can't believe you're home!"

We fell into one another's arms, hugging so hard I thought one of us would crack a rib. I let go and wiped away the tears with my fingers until she handed me a napkin. "I got your message from Ciara. I was sorry you couldn't make it to the party yesterday."

Her hand was placed on her slim hip as she swung the towel in her hand around in a circle. "One of my part-timers called in sick, so I was stuck working until close."

"It was a great party. The best part was my giving Fiona a bloody nose."

"What? Wait. Before you explain, let's have tea and a treat."

I choose a piece of tiramisu cheesecake, which she placed on a white and yellow plate painted with a bright yellow sunflower, matching the theme of the bakery. "This place is amazing, Re. Your love of baking paid off."

Reanna's green eyes glowed. "It's a dream come true. Mind you, there are days I can't help but wonder what I was thinking, but I've been open for two years, and things are going really well." She brought over a tray with a pot of tea and my dessert, pouring us each a cup.

"I can see your personality in everything." From the yellow painted crates in the corner with faux cakes and pies to the bright yellow walls. The green wooden tables were placed throughout with a sunflower painted on each one. "You painted these sunflowers, didn't you?"

"I did. You know I love to paint almost as much as I love to bake." She smiled. The only thing I didn't do was the pictures on the walls. Those were my brother, Conor."

I took a bite of my dessert and almost moaned. This wasn't made with just cream cheese. "You made this with mascarpone, didn't you?" I pointed to the plate as I took another bite.

"How did you know?" She smiled.

"Because it's much creamier than I'm used to. It's excellent!"

I glanced around at the framed photos on the walls. There were quite a few of them, but there were also some empty spaces in between. "Why the blank spaces?"

"We get a lot of tourists, and they love them, so I sell them for ten to thirty euros each and split the money with Conor. It's a win-win for both of us. However, he's getting so busy with photography jobs, he hasn't had time to replace them."

I got up and looked at them closer. Some were black and white; some were color. They were 8x10s, all wooden frames—some matted, some not. Most were of local landmarks such as St. Mary's Church, Dooley Castle, and pictures taken at Dooley beach. I also recognized pictures taken down the coast at the Cliffs of Moher. They were well worth the price.

"Can you believe my brat of a brother would find something he was good at?"

"He was quite the troublemaker from what I remember." I walked from one to the next admiring them. I would have to remember this if and when I ever buy my own place.

"Yes. He's twenty-five now. Can you believe it?"

"That makes me feel old. I remember him as a gangly teenager following Ciara around."

"The pictures sell really well. He's actually the official photographer of the gala on Saturday night."

"Mum hired a photographer?" That was surprising. I didn't think Mum would spend the extra money.

"I think it was the event planner who did it, actually. Whoever it was, Conor is ecstatic."

I sat back down to my cheesecake just as the bell over the door clanged, and a cool breeze blew in. Reanna's smile left her face when she saw who it was. I glanced around, and my smile disappeared as well.

I heard Reanna let out a sigh. "Margery, this is a surprise. What are you doing here? You said you'd never take a step in here." She crossed her arms in front of her. "I believe you used the words 'the place where that bitch sells sweet crap.'"

"Yes, well, I'm surprised myself, but I'm here to speak to Miss Prissy there," she pointed at me and glared. "I just want you to know it will not work."

I swallowed the cheesecake and said, "What won't work?"

She leaned into me until we were almost nose to nose. "I know you're trying to get Dillon to break up with me, but it will not happen. Do you hear me?"

I laid my hand on her upper chest and pushed her a few inches away. "I am not my brother's keeper. If he decides he wants you out of his life, it is his decision, not mine."

I heard Reanna chuckling as she got up and walked back behind the counter.

Margery's eyes widened. "We'll see who has the last laugh when I become your sister-in-law, and I'm the lady of the manor!" She took a few steps back, and I could breathe again.

I bit my lip to stop myself from laughing. Looking at her closely, I could see the tears forming in her eyes, and I felt a tad bit of guilt. Well, only a small tad.

"Really? Well, good luck because I don't think that's what Dillon has in mind." I refilled my teacup.

I felt a swoosh of air as she turned around and stomped out of the store.

As soon as the door closed, Reanna came back out from behind the counter, shaking her head. "She is unbelievable!" She sat back down.

"Why on earth did she move back here?" I took my last bite of cheesecake, wondering how much I would hate myself if I ordered another one.

"Did you hear she was a suspect in her husband's death? Too bad they couldn't prove it. It would be nice to see her behind bars." Reanna sat back down.

"Let's talk about more pleasant things. Are you coming to the gala on Saturday?"

She grinned. "I am. Sean Fuller, the local vet, asked me to go. He has a ten-year-old daughter who is a sweety."

"That's great! Could he be Mr. Right?" I warmed up her tea.

She shrugged. "More like Mr. Right Now." She grinned. "He's a delightful man, but there just isn't any spark. You know?"

I nodded, thinking of Liam.

"Well, I look forward to meeting him." I took a sip of the cinnamon tea.

We spoke for a few more minutes until some additional customers came in. I spent several minutes playing with my new phone, texting everyone on my contact list my new phone number. I waved at Reanna as I left, promising to catch up at the gala, and I headed out.

My next stop was at the bank, where I had all of my funds transferred from my previous bank. I left with both a credit card and a debit card tucked into my purse to find out it was raining, and I'd forgotten my umbrella. I noticed a store across the square with a sleek black evening gown in the window, so I dashed in there. I had just shaken the raindrops off when I heard a French accent ask, "How may I help you?"

The woman was tall and thin, and the first word that came to mind was "regal." Her ebony hair was in a bun, and her makeup was perfect, highlighting her high cheekbones. She could have been a model in her younger years.

"Ah, yes. I'm looking for an evening gown for Saturday night." I looked around the store. There were several displays with dresses, but I didn't see any gowns.

"I have a few options. Did you see the gown in the window?" She pointed.

"I did, but I was hoping for something a little less— black, maybe?"

She looked me up and down and let out a sigh. "I have one dress that I had on hold for a customer, but she hasn't come back for it. It will definitely look much better on you than on her. Wait here."

Not only did the store offer clothes, but they also offered shoes and purses. This must be the dress shop Fiona was talking about.

"Here, what do you think of this?"

If it was possible to fall in love with a dress, this was it. It was light blue, and the material sparkled in the light. It was low in the front with silver piping that crossed at the breasts; the piping continued down to the slit in front.

"It's gorgeous! May I try it on?"

"Come this way." She led me toward the back of the store to a dressing room. I quickly undressed, unzipped it, and slid it over my head. I looked in the mirror and knew this was the dress for me. I couldn't get it all the way zipped, so I walked out into the shop.

"I'm sorry, what is your name?" I asked as I turned my back toward her.

She zipped me up as she answered. "Jeannette Dubois." She directed me to a three-way mirror with a stage in front of it. I could even compete with Fiona in this dress!

"It looks lovely on you! Do you have shoes? It may have to be shortened."

I had to think. Even if my stuff arrived on time, I didn't think I had anything that would work. "Not really. Do you have anything?"

"What size?"

"Eight."

She looked at me, and I smiled. I tried to remember my European size but drew a blank. "Sorry, it's been a while since I've been back here.

"Eight, American?"

I nodded, still not being able to take my eyes off the dress. I turned in every direction and glanced at the mirror.

Madame Dubois came back a minute later with a pair of open-toed silver sandals that wrapped around the ankle. They would go perfectly with the dress.

I hopped off the stage, ignoring her gathered brows, and sat down in a chair. She handed me the shoes, and I slipped them on and stood up.

"The dress will still need to be shortened but not much. It fits well. Don't you think, mademoiselle?"

I looked in the mirror again and smiled.

"Oui." Using the small amount of French I remembered from school.

When she took down my name and address to have it delivered, she said, "Oh, you are the child of Deidre and Joseph?"

"I am. I just arrived yesterday. I've moved back from the United States."

"Your parents are lovely people. I will be there too on Saturday, along with my husband, Felipe." She motioned for me to twirl around in the mirror.

A few minutes later, I was back in my street clothes and was at the counter.

"Do you require anything else?" She waved her hand at the jewelry counter.

By the time I left, I'd picked up a few pieces of jewelry, two sweaters, and two dresses, one of which I was planning to wear that evening for dinner with the grandparents. I tried not to flinch at the total. "I look forward to seeing you on Saturday night and meeting your husband."

She waved to me as I left and noticed Margery across the street just coming out of the bank. I saw her walk into the dress shop as I unlocked Dad's car and added my packages to the trunk, ah, boot, and headed home.

The block dress I'd chosen for dinner hit just above the knee. The back and sides were black, but the front had a block of white, showing off my slim waist. I added my black heels, and the pearl necklace and earrings my grandparents had given me when I graduated college.

I made it downstairs just as the doorbell rang. Higgins opened it just as I got to the bottom of the stairs.

My grandparents walked in, Gram first, and gave me a hug.

"I've missed you, lassie! Welcome home." I felt tears in my eyes as she held me at arm's length. "You're too thin, but that dress is lovely."

I hugged her again. "I've missed you, Gram."

"Hey, what about me?" asked a gruff voice from behind her.

I laughed. "I missed you too, Gramps." I waited until he was in the room before giving him a hug. He was well over six feet tall, and I always felt like I was hugging a big ole' teddy bear whenever I hugged him. James and Bridget O'Leary were both in their eighties and lived about a mile away on a small patch of land on the river where

Gramps spent his time fishing and Gram taking care of Gramps.

"Let me take your coats," I said as they moved into the parlor. It was then I noticed the cane.

"Gramps, since when have you been using a cane?" I asked, glaring at my mum.

"Don't look at me like that. I didn't know he was using a cane," she said as she glared at her dad.

"It's nothing. I had a bit of a fall—"

"A fall?" her mum asked, who glared at her own mum.

Gram looked at Gramps and said, "I told you we should have told them."

Gramps took a deep breath and said, "It was nothing, really. I tripped and fell and bruised my knee. The doctor suggested I use a cane for a week or two."

I couldn't help but smile at all the glaring. I took my granddad's arm and pulled him into the parlor, where he sat down on the couch.

"Why don't you sit down and I'll get you a drink. What do you prefer?"

"I'll take a gin and tonic, dear."

"Gram?"

"Nothing, dear. I'm driving."

The parents both asked for ginger ale and brandy, which sounded good to me as well, so we all sat down and chatted.

"Molly, did you master the gift I sent you at Christmas?" Gran asked.

I grinned. "I did, but it took me a few months of practice. I still can't believe you bought that for me."

Gran just smiled, and Mum asked me, "What's she talking about, dear?"

Before I could answer, Gran said, "Nothing for you to concern yourself with, Deidre." She sat back farther into the couch. "So, how are the arrangements for the gala coming along?" she asked Mum, winking at me.

The next quarter-hour was spent listening to Mum discuss all the work that had gone into the gala and how much there was to do. Mrs. Jones saved us by announcing dinner was ready.

Chapter 6

The next day started with cloudy skies, and I woke up more tired than when I went to bed. Jet lag is always worse for me on the second day, so I pulled the covers up and tried to go back to sleep.

I woke up to someone shaking me. I turned around to see Fiona standing next to my bed.

"Wake up, snoozer!"

She'd put her hair into a ponytail and was wearing a bandage on her nose. I couldn't help but smile.

"Don't you dare! This is your fault I'm like this. And I'll have you know, it's very hard to sleep with a bruised nose. And if I can't sleep, you don't get to sleep either," she said as she whipped the covers off me.

I sat up on my elbows. "I am very sorry, Fi. Does it hurt much?" I could see yellow and purple skin under the bandage.

"Move over." She smiled and crawled into bed with me. "It did at first, but not so much anymore."

I went to touch it, and she stopped me. "It doesn't hurt as long as you don't touch it!"

I put my hand down and my head on her shoulder. "Do you forgive me?" I asked, throwing the blanket over both of us.

"I guess so."

"What are you doing here, anyway? Shouldn't you be at work?" I looked over at her.

"My boss felt sorry for me, so he gave me the rest of the week off. He also thought it was funny that the sister I wanted to spend time with is the one who almost broke my nose."

"Well, it's not as bad as the time I slammed your hand in the car door, is it?" I asked.

"No, or the time you broke my jaw."

"I didn't break your jaw; you broke your jaw riding your bike."

"Yes, but you were the one outside refusing to come in when Mum called. Mum sent me out to get you, and I hit that large rock and flew over the handlebars."

I laughed. "Yes, but the wonderful thing about it was we found out you needed glasses."

We were both giggling when the door flew open, and Mum stepped in. We both became silent.

"What is this? Fiona, I sent you to wake your sister up, not get in bed with her. And why do you have the bandage back on your nose? Didn't the doctor say you could take it off?"

I picked up my pillow and hit her with it. "What? You don't have to wear it any longer? You just did that so I'd feel worse than I already do!"

She laughed as she scooted out of bed, tearing off the bandage as she did so. "And I bet you used makeup to give your nose those colors, didn't you?" I said as I threw another pillow at her.

"Ow! No—those are real. I can't believe you just threw that at me! Mum—"

"Don't Mum me. You two need to get up and get going. Molly, your boxes have arrived. They're in the garage, but I need both of you downstairs to help."

I took a quick shower, threw on jeans and a tee-shirt, and headed downstairs. There were people all over the place dusting and vacuuming and moving things around. I went to the kitchen to see if I could get a cup of tea when I heard Mrs. Jones barking at two young women. One was kneading some dough, the other stirring a pot. I tiptoed in to see if there was any tea brewing. I'd almost made it to the stove when I heard, "Molly Colleen, what are you doing?"

I felt like I was five again when Mrs. Jones caught me trying to sneak her ginger cookies.

I swallowed and pointed to the teapot. "Just trying to get a cup of tea," I said, looking down and putting my hands together in front of me.

She laughed as she opened the cupboard and handed me a cup and saucer.

"There you go, child. Help yourself."

I looked at the teacup and asked, "Is there a larger cup around someplace?"

She looked at me, her brows furrowed, and said, "I'm making tea for your mum and sister. It will be delivered shortly. You can refill it then."

"Yes, ma'am," I said, filling my tea and scooting out of the room. It wasn't until I tasted it when I realized I'd forgotten to add sugar. Damn!

Anna, the regular maid, was busy working on the ballroom, so Mum assigned Fiona and me all the guest bedrooms. We were to make sure they all had fresh sheets on the beds and to open the windows to air out the rooms. We were to also check each bathroom to make sure they all had fresh towels and were clean.

By lunchtime, we were both famished and knackered and had only finished half the rooms.

As we ambled down the stairs to lunch, I said to Fiona, "They have child labor laws in America. Do they have them here?"

Fiona smiled. "We do, but we're adults, so it's not child labor. It's slavery."

Mum was passing the stairs just then but didn't stop. She just smiled and said, "You're going to be late for lunch if you don't hurry. But I can always have bread and water brought up to you later. Isn't that what slaves eat?" We both giggled as she walked away.

Lunch was soup and sandwiches, and if Dad was around, he didn't make an appearance, probably preferring to stay away from the house and sharing Stewart's lunch down at the barn.

"Mum, I forgot to mention my friend, Bethany Clark, is going to stop by. Is that okay with you?"

"Bethany? Which one is she?" she asked as she took a bite of her sandwich.

"She's the server from the café, remember? The one who told ole' Mr. Weatherby, he needed to have a website for the café."

"I remember her now. She's part of the catering staff for the gala."

Fiona nodded as she finished her soup and took a sandwich from the enormous stack set in the middle of the table. "She wanted to check out the house before tomorrow. She likes to learn the layout of where she's working in advance. She normally would just arrive early, but since it was here, I invited her to come today."

I nodded. "That makes sense, especially this house. It can get confusing if you've never been here before." I looked at Fi. "Does she work catering events often?"

"When she gets the opportunity. She works at the café as well as the Golden Goose Restaurant, but catering pays much better."

It wasn't until much later when I went downstairs for some tea that I met Fiona's friend Bethany. She was a lot older than I expected her to be, which was close to forty. Casually dressed in jeans and a sweatshirt, she had bright eyes and a ready smile. Fiona introduced me as "the sister who almost broke her nose."

There were tea and cookies laid out on the table, so I helped myself to a cup of tea and added the required sugar. "It's nice to meet you, Bethany. Have you two known each other long?" I added a cookie to my plate and sat down on the couch across from them.

Fiona looked at Bethany and asked, "About a year, I think?"

I took a sip of tea. "Where did you meet?"

Fiona laughed. "At the café where she works. We just started talking and realized we have a lot in common, and it grew from there."

We talked until our tea was cold, and Mum gave us the evil eye. Fi showed Bethany around the ballroom and how to get from there to the kitchen while I finished up the last few bedrooms. I returned downstairs to find the two of them at the front door. Bethany gave Fiona a hug and waved to me as she left.

Fiona was smiling as she closed the door. "She seems like a nice lady. You really like her, don't you?"

"I do. Ever since Mindy moved away, I haven't really had a best friend, so it's nice to have someone to hang out with."

My heart sank. "Does that mean you won't be hanging out with me?"

"Of course not! I will hang out with you as much as you can stand me." She looked at her watch. "I was thinking we could go visit Mrs. Riley. Do you have time?"

"Yes, just let me get my jacket."

We were walking out the door when we spotted Bethany walking back from the gardens. Fi looked at her and smiled. "What are you still doing here?"

"I misplaced my keys. Remember when I pulled out the tissue from my pocket? I must have dropped them then." She jangled her keys at us. "I found them, so all is not lost." She walked to her car. "I'll talk to you all later!" She got in and drove away.

The sky was full of mean-looking clouds, but I could see the sun trying to peek through. This time though, I remembered my umbrella.

It didn't take much to talk Fiona into making a stop at Reanna's bakery to pick up a treat to take to Mrs. Riley. We turned the corner onto High Street, and I spotted the Book Bin on the corner, right next door to Dooley's café. Looking at the red awning of the bookstore brought back pleasant memories of working there during the summer months and holiday breaks back when I was in school. We parked in the parking lot at the back of the store and made our way to the front door. The bell rang as we walked in, and I heard a voice from the back yell, "I'll be out in a minute!"

The place had changed little since the last time I was here. The windows still displayed the current bestsellers and souvenirs from the area to bring in the tourists. The displays of local cookbooks, aprons, magnets, and stuffed leprechauns were placed on shelves in front, with books of all genres behind them. I headed to the mystery section when I heard a voice say, "Molly Quinn, is that you?"

I turned to see Mrs. Riley shuffling up the aisle toward us. Her short, gray hair had little pin curls, her compact body dressed in a tee-shirt and jeans with her apron tied around her thick waist.

I went to her and enveloped her in a hug. "Mrs. R., how are you?" I couldn't help but smile.

We let each other go, and then she gave Fiona a quick hug. "Oh, my goodness. What happened to your face?"

"I ran into a suitcase with Molly on the other end, Mrs. Riley. Nothing to be too concerned about." She turned to me and stuck out her tongue. Luckily, Mrs. R. had turned her back.

"Oh, so it was Molly's fault, was it? You always tried to cover for her." She winked at me and said, "I just put the kettle on. It should be ready shortly." She noticed the box I was carrying and asked, "What is this now?"

I handed her the box. "We stopped on the way here and picked up some treats. I hope you don't mind."

"Why would I mind, dear?" She opened the box and said, "Ooh, my favorites! Reanna must have told you how much I love her lemon bars. They're so scrumptious and will taste wonderful with the tea."

She looked at Fiona and said, "Dearie, can you please lock the door and put the closed sign up. We can dash in the back and have our tea with no interruptions."

Fiona did as Mrs. Riley asked and then joined us in the kitchen area at the back of the store.

It was a medium-sized room with a small refrigerator, microwave, stove, and counter. There was a door with a pink curtain I remembered led outside to a small yard. She motioned to the wood table in the corner with the four mismatched chairs. "Sit down there. Tea will be ready in a minute."

"Can I help you, Mrs. Riley?" I asked. She was moving a lot slower than she used to. I'd written quite a few letters to her when I first went to America, but as time went by, there were other things to keep me busy, and the letters stopped. I thought of her often, though. I just never followed up. I really was a selfish person.

"That would be lovely." She nodded toward a cupboard door. "Can you get out the small plates for the dessert?" Oh, and Fiona, you know where the cups are. Could you pull out three?"

Fiona and I did as she asked, bringing them all to the table. "Oh, I forgot the sugar."

I stood up and gathered it from the cupboard, setting it down on the table.

"You might not need that, dear. This flavor is quite sweet already." She added the water to the kettle and then added the tea bags. "I'm almost done here. I hope you like it. I try to change things up now and again. At my age, trying new tea flavors is as good as it gets." She smiled as she put the tray down on the table. "Let's give that a few minutes to steep." She sat down in the chair across from me, next to Fiona.

"You look wonderful, Mrs. Riley." The chairs were hard, and I moved around, trying to get comfortable.

"Oh, thank you, lassie, but I'm getting old. Thinking of retiring, I am. Know anyone interested in buying a bookstore?" She laughed as she poured the tea. "This is orange and honey. I hope you like it. It's one of my favorites."

The aroma of orange hit my nose as I took a sip. It was good, and the honey did give it a sweet taste. "You seem to get a lot of business," I remarked as I added one teaspoon of sugar.

"I do. Surprisingly, really with all the electronic books out there, but kids do still love to read, and a lot of them can't afford one of those electronic readers, so I keep busy."

I took her hand and asked, "Is there anything I can do for you, Mrs. R.?"

She smiled, showing her crooked teeth. "You are such a dear. Those days when you worked for me and Henry were grand times, weren't they?" She smiled. She was quiet then. I imagined she had gone back in time with her beloved Henry. She and Mr. Riley were always laughing and joking with each other. I never heard either of them ever raise their voice.

She sighed and looked at me. "I'm okay. You know, since the Lord above never blessed Henry and me with children, you are the closest we ever had." She took my hand, then Fiona's. "And when you left, Fiona here always took time to come in and check on me." She looked at us. "You're both such delightful girls."

I could feel tears forming in my eyes, but refused to give in, instead, clearing my throat. "I'm glad you're doing well. You look great." I took another sip of tea, enjoying the citrus scent as it tingled my nose.

"Thank you, dear, but I'm tired. My mind isn't what it used to be, and it gets harder and harder to do the books. I want to retire to the seaside and rest my weary bones." She took a lemon bar from the box and set it on her plate.

"But you already live by the seaside. You didn't sell it, did you? I asked.

"No, dear. But I wouldn't mind being someplace warmer. My ole' bones can't take the chill like they used to."

I took one of the lemon bars and offered one to Fiona. She took one and added it to her plate.

"Have there been any offers?" I took a bite and had to hold back the groan. The tart lemon hit my tongue and then melted in my mouth. Reanna was a genius.

"Only one, and I refuse to sell to that, that, hussy!"

Fiona choked on her lemon bar, and my eyes went wide. "Mrs. Riley! I don't think I've ever heard you say an unpleasant word about anyone. Who are you talking about?" I glanced at Fiona, who shrugged.

"Margery Denton. She made me an offer, and a poor one at that. The Dooley Business Association would have my head if I sold to her. She'd be sticking her nose in everyone's business!"

I looked at Fiona, but she just shrugged.

"I'm not that fond of her either, but what did she do to make you dislike her so much?" I asked.

"She's just a menace. Always eavesdropping on people's conversations, ordering books and never picking them up. I would call and leave messages, or remind her when I'd see her on the street." She looked at me. "You remember the rule, don't you?"

I nodded. "Customers have seven days to pick up their orders, or they go on the shelf, right?" I asked with a smile.

"Exactly! Most people abide, but not Miss Goody Two-Shoes. She wouldn't arrive until after they'd sold, then come in and throw a fit because I sold them to someone else. Plus, no one likes her. Why would you buy books from someone you don't like?"

"I can see how that would upset you, but why wouldn't you sell to her? Isn't that better than having to delay your retirement?" Fiona asked.

Mrs. Riley picked out another lemon bar and placed it on her plate. "It's not just that. She seems to be after every man in town, doesn't matter if they're married or not." She looked at each of us. "I hear she has her claws into your brother these days. Tell him to run for the hills." She took a bite of her lemon bar, shaking her head.

"He's trying, Mrs. R., but he's having problems getting her to listen," I also took a second lemon bar out of the box and placed it on my plate.

"Good luck to 'im," she said.

Fiona looked at her and asked, "Are you coming to the gala on Saturday?"

She grinned. "I am. Mr. Owen, one of my customers and a good friend, is escorting me. I'm looking so forward to it. It reminds me of the old times with the dances up at the grand hall."

We left shortly after, changing the closed sign to open. As I glanced back at the door, I could see three people who had been sitting at one of the café tables get up and walk into the store, and I left smiling.

On our way back to the parents' house, Fiona said, "It seems we've found another person not too fond of Margery."

"Margery does have the spectacular knack of being able to rub people the wrong way. I think she enjoys it."

"Maybe a divorce and becoming a widow changed her somehow—made her more bitter."

"Maybe, but if I get that way when I'm old, please shoot me."

Fiona laughed as she pulled into the driveway. "Oh, don't worry. I will."

I left the car, waving to her as she followed the circle drive and continued out to the road.

Chapter 7

Friday morning brought more clouds, but I could see a bit of sunshine trying to peek through. Anytime the sun chose to shine is considered a marvelous day in Ireland. I dressed in a pair of navy-blue ankle pants, a collared shirt, grabbed my sweater and headed downstairs.

My parents were sitting comfortably at the breakfast table, Dad in a suit, reading the morning paper, and Mum with a scowl on her face, glaring at Dad. Uh oh. What's going on now, I wondered as I scooped out some scrambled eggs and a slice of ham from the sideboard and set my plate down at the table. Mum was already pouring me a cup of tea, then picked up the sugar bowl, practically slamming it down in front of me.

I placed my napkin on my lap and stirred sugar into my tea. "Good morning?"

Mum slammed down her teacup and glared at my dad, and I heard a deep sigh as Dad folded up his paper and laid it beside him. "Deidre, I told you I can't get out of going to court this morning. I should be back by the time our guests arrive."

Ah, that was the reason. I looked at Mum. There were black rings under her eyes that her makeup couldn't hide. She always gets like this when we have a large gathering. She loves to entertain but hates the prep work.

"You'd better be, Joseph, because you know who will be the first to arrive—your Aunt Agatha. She's hated me from the day we were married. She will come in here and find fault with everything!"

"Aunt Agatha's coming?" We all tried to stay out of her way, as she gave everyone a hard time. "That's not such a bad thing, is it?" I smiled.

Mum turned her scowl to me, and I quickly quenched my smile.

"Of course, she's coming. And probably that horrid granddaughter of hers as well." Mum picked up her teacup and sipped, then set it quickly back down, a horrid look on her face. I got up and got her a fresh cup and set it before her.

"Thank you, dear," she said as she took a sip.

"Doreen is coming too? She's the mousy one, isn't she?" I sat back down, reaching into my memory, and coming up with a short woman, a little pudgy with glasses. "She's my age, right, maybe a little older? Did she ever get married?" I took a bite of my eggs.

Mum looked at me, her glare turning to just one eyebrow lifting.

"I'll take that as a no." I retreated to my plate to cut my ham and took a bite. I really missed American bacon.

"No one is that desperate. She's Aunt Agatha's 'companion.' Who has companions these days? Didn't that go out with after the Great War?" Mum took another sip of her tea.

I looked at her and then looked at my dad, who shrugged. I set my fork down with a clatter.

"Okay, Mum. What's going on? You rarely act like this. Is something wrong? Should I add some brandy to your tea?" I winked at Dad.

"No, I don't want any brandy in my tea. It's way too early for that, but once Aunt Agatha comes, keep it handy. I'm sorry I'm being such a—"

"Shrew?" I said.

"Pain," Dad said.

Mum glared at us as she sat back in her chair. "I don't know what's wrong. I just have a strange feeling about this event." She shook her head.

"Oh, are your Spidey senses tingling?" I smiled "My what?"

I looked at the blank look on her face and turned to Dad. His looked the same. "Seriously? Neither of you has watched the Spider-Man movies?" I picked up my fork again. "Wow. Okay, we're supposed to have fairy blood, right? It must be your fairy blood tingling. Well, blood probably doesn't tingle. How about bubbling? Is your fairy blood bubbling?" I chuckled.

Mum looked at me like I'd grown two heads. "What on earth are you talking about?"

"Strange how?" I asked, giving up on the metaphors.

She sat back up straighter. "I don't know. Just a strange feeling of—doom? I'm not sure if that's the right word. I just know the last time I had this feeling; Dad Kearney fell off the back patio and broke his ankle."

I laughed. "I remember that." Mum turned and scowled at me.

Dad chimed in. "Dear, Dad Kearney fell off the patio and broke his ankle because he'd had too much to drink. Don't you remember? He started singing "Danny Boy" and was trying to climb up on the table." He smiled as he took a drink of tea.

"I remember he had a delightful voice." I took another bite of food, ignoring the scowl I could feel coming from the other side of the table. After I'd finished my breakfast, I pushed back my chair and looked at Mum. "So, what is on the agenda for this morning?"

"The florist should be here shortly. I want a fresh vase of flowers in the bedrooms being used for guests. If you could take care of that for me, I would appreciate it."

"I can do that. I was hoping to go to the festival this afternoon if that's okay with you?" I looked at her, hopefully.

"That's fine, as long as your dad's home. If not, you get to help me greet our guests." The scowl moved back to Dad, who got up out of his chair, walked over to Mum, and kissed her on the cheek.

"I'll be back in plenty of time," he said as he walked from the room.

The flowers arrived early in the day, and I placed them in the bedrooms soon-to-be slept in, along with a little welcome package Mum had coordinated for everyone with a small bottle of Irish Whiskey, a bottle of wine, and cookies freshly made by Mrs. Jones. She truly was a wonderful hostess. Dad appeared right after lunch, so I was free to go to the festival.

Since I had some time before going into town, I took a walk around the gardens. The patio surrounds the back of the house, so I exited the double doors from the breakfast room. The wind was blowing from the west, bringing the salt air inland to tingle my nose. I looked out at the vast land, proud of the fact it was Quinn land as far as the eye could see. Although obscured this time of year by trees, I knew there were sheep to the north, cattle to the south, and out beyond the garden, the Pacific Ocean.

I headed to my favorite part of the garden, where Mum had planted her roses. I had missed the flower festival this year by two weeks, where once again, mother's roses took first place. As I looked at them now, still in bloom, I could see why. The bright colors of red, blue, orange, and purple were pleasant to the eye as I sat down on the wooden bench and took a deep breath. What a gorgeous day. I smiled at the butterflies dancing around the flowers, and the birds chirping to one another as they flew from tree to the ground to look for food, then back up into the trees.

I observed three men working on the three-tier fountain located in the center of the garden. The fountain was currently turned off, but two men had a huge bucket between them, along with long-handled scrub brushes, cleaning off the dirt and bird droppings, and the third one was walking behind them with a hose, rinsing the fountain and inspecting it as they moved. They reminded me of synchronized swimmers as they carefully circled the fountain, making sure it gleamed in time for the gala.

After a few minutes, I continued my walk around the perimeter of the garden, avoiding the area where the fountain was located. I thought I saw something shining in the dirt ahead of me, but before I could see something shining in the dirt and I vaguely wondered what it could be when my phone dinged. My first text message on my brand-new phone! Silly to be excited about such things, especially when I read it. It was from Dillon.

"Hey, sis, can u come help us at the beer tent?"

"Sure. B there soon."

"Thx,"

I left the garden to see if I could borrow Dad's car. I found him in the cattle barn, but rather than answering, he threw me the keys. Of course, I missed them, so bent down to pick them up, and hit my head on the wheelbarrow. I hadn't realized it was so close. I was rubbing my head as I walked to the car and then drove into town.

I parked behind the pub and made my way to the front door. Pounding sounds, along with chatter and laughter, greeted me on High Street as the entire street prepared for the festival. The street was blocked off to traffic, and tables and tents were set up all along the road. The beer tent practically at the pub's front door. I could hear laughing coming from inside the tent, so I headed there first.

The long tent consisted of long tables covered with tablecloths set up as makeshift bars on each end of the tent. The farthest one had already been set up. The other one was being worked on by none other than the bartender I'd met the day I arrived. What was his name? Scott—that's it. Four other people were setting up round tables and chairs.

"Molly, isn't it?" He smiled as he moved liquor from a box to the table behind the bar.

"It is. I'm looking for my brothers. They texted wanting help."

"Dillon was here a minute ago." He looked around. "He must be inside with Aiden."

"Thanks," I waved and walked the few steps from the tent to the pub.

It took a minute for my eyes to adjust from the bright sunshine to the darkness of the interior. It was much quieter in here, so I made my way to the office in the back near the restrooms.

Aiden was sitting at the desk, and Dillon was in the chair in front of it, his hands behind his head, the chair tipped back. I grinned. "You're going to fall one of these days," I said.

He put the legs of the chair back on the floor. "Now you sound like Mum."

I wrinkled my nose, "I did, didn't I?" I pulled up another chair and sat down. "What's up? Do you really need help, or were you just saving me from a day of chores? Mum's in a rare mood today." I rolled my eyes.

Dillon looked at Aiden, tilting his head toward me. "See, I told you she'd be going nuts."

Aiden shook his head, "It's only been two days. How can she be driving you nutty already?"

"It's been, well, two and a half days, but it feels longer. It's the gala driving her crazy, so in turn, she's driving me and Dad crazy."

I looked from one brother to the other. They were both dressed in jeans and tee-shirts: Dillon's black and tight to show off his muscles and flat stomach, Aiden in navy blue, looser to hide his thickening middle. Ciara must be a good cook.

Aiden was sitting in his chair, leaning back, his hands behind his head, "Ciara is looking forward to the gala, though. It's been a while since we've gotten away from the kids for an evening."

I thought of Kayleigh's smiling face. "I really need to get over and see them soon."

"You're welcome anytime. Kaleigh has talked about you nonstop since she met you, so yes, please make the time." Aiden smiled.

Dillon had his chair tilted back again. I pretended to look at my nails as I said to him, "So, according to Margery, you're ready to propose. How are you going to do it? A hot air balloon ride? A romantic stroll on the beach?" I tried to keep my face serious, but couldn't keep the grin from coming through.

His chair hit the floor with a bang, and he knocked his knee against the desk. "Ow! That hurt," His hand flew over his knee, and he rubbed it. "What?" His eyes widened, and then his mouth gaped open.

"I ran into Margery yesterday, and she informed me how I was about to become her sister-in-law."

He stood up and started pacing. "What am I going to do? She is driving me crazy. Married? I don't want to get married, let alone get married to her!"

Aiden, always the level-headed one, replied, "Dillon, calm down. Have you told her you want to break up with her, or are you just ignoring her phone calls, hoping she'll get the hint, like you usually do?" We watched as Dillon's face turned pink. "You eejit! You haven't actually told her you want to break up, have you?" Aiden shook his head.

Dillon rubbed his hand over his face and sat down again. "Most women know how I do things!" He lowered his head, then lifted it, eyeing us both. "I guess I need to tell her, don't I?"

I had to laugh at the look on his face. "Dillon, you're not going to the gallows. My goodness, just talk to the woman!"

He looked at me, his green eyes pleading, "I don't suppose you'd talk to her for me?"

"Oh, no. You get to take care of this fiasco on your own, big brother."

He bent over and put his head in his hands just as his phone rang. He looked at the caller and groaned, showing us the screen. It said, "Margery." He got up as he answered, leaving the office.

I looked at Aiden. "Do you think he'll ever fall in love?"

"I've only ever seen him close once, and he got so scared he ran and broke her heart."

"Really? Who was that?" I didn't recall my brother every falling in love with anyone.

"It was while you were in America. It was your lovely friend, Reanna."

"Reanna? Really? I just saw her yesterday. She didn't say a word about it."

"She's one in a million, I must admit. I think for him, she's the one that got away." He sat back in his chair, tapping a pen on his desk.

"She'll be at the gala tomorrow with a date."

"Really? Who?"

"I can't recall his name, but he's the local vet."

"Ah, I'd heard we'd gotten a replacement. Ciara had to take Charlie in for his shots."

"Charlie is still alive? Wow, he has to be getting old. He was old when I left." Charlie was an Irish setter Dad had found abandoned and brought home. Mum refused to keep it, so my brother took him in when the twins were just little.

"He's only seven. He has a few years left in him."

"So, do you really need my help?" I really didn't feel like being stuck in a tent the whole evening.

"We can probably use your help later. Remember how to tend bar?"

"You're talking to the wrong sister, Aiden. It was Fiona who worked here during her holidays. I worked at the bookstore. However, I think even I can handle pouring beer."

He laughed as Dillon came in and slammed the door behind him. "That woman! She is impossible! I could kill her. You know that?"

We both looked at him and asked, "What happened?"

"She refuses to believe me!"

"How can she not believe you?" I asked bewildered.

He pointed his finger at me. "She thinks this is all your fault, that you never liked her, and you've talked me into this, and if we stay together, I'll change my mind."

I looked at them both and said, "Wait, she thinks this is my fault?"

He nodded.

"How is this my fault?"

"It's not. I don't know how she comes up with these things." He shook his head. "She was already in a nasty mood. She went to go pick up her dress, and the lady sold it to someone else."

I grinned. "Oh, well, that may be my fault. If it's the dress I'm thinking of, that was me."

Aiden started laughing, and Dillon started pacing, rubbing the back of his neck and muttering under his breath.

"Dillon, I'm sorry! I needed a dress, and Madame Dubois said the person she was holding it for didn't pick it up. Besides, I was told it looks much better on me." I laughed.

Dillon glared at both of us, turning toward the door. The look was so much like our mum I had to grin. "I'll take the beer kegs out to the tent," he said as he left.

Aiden and I laughed as the door slammed shut.

Chapter 8

I left Aiden in his office, dealing with paperwork, and went out to the tent to see if I could be of any help. They had set the tables up, and most everyone was standing around gabbing, so I left, stopping by several shops, picking up a few toiletries and saying hello to people I hadn't seen since I left. My stomach started growling, so I stopped by the bookstore to see if I could bring Mrs. Riley some lunch. There was an elderly woman behind the counter I didn't recognize who explained she was Beatrice's friend and neighbor who helped her occasionally. After making sure Mrs. Riley wasn't ill, I made my way to the café for lunch, where I was pleased to see Bethany was working.

There was a sign stating to seat yourself, but I flagged Bethany down to ask which section she was working. She pointed, and I had a seat.

"Hiya! What are you doing here? Isn't your Mum keeping you busy enough?" she asked as she put a paper placemat in front of me.

"Oh, she is, but I received a request for help from my brothers, who don't need me yet, so I've been wandering around town. I had planned on taking lunch to Mrs. Riley, but she's not working. Is that usual?" I asked, looking at her as she handed me the menu.

She nodded. "She always takes Fridays off. She works too hard. I keep telling her to hire me part-time, but she insists she can handle it alone."

"Another job? Where do you find the time?" You really need to look for that accounting job and settle down."

She just smiled and asked, "What would you like to drink?"

"I'll have an Arnold Palmer, please," I said as I perused the menu.

"I'm sorry, a what?" She looked at me with raised eyebrows.

I looked at her and grinned. "Sorry, it must not have made it across the pond. It's half-iced tea and half lemonade." I glanced at the beverages offered. "I see you have both. Is it possible to combine them?"

She laughed as she wrote on her order pad. "Sure. I'll get that right out to you. An Arnold Palmer, I'll remember that." She stuck the pad and pen in her apron. "I'll be back in a jiffy with your drink and take your order."

I decided on soup and a ham-and-cheese toasty, looking toward the front of the café for their list of soups, my eyes lighting up when I spotted my favorite listed. As I sat there, I watched droves of people come in and sit down. I could see four servers on hand, all running around and taking orders. Glancing at the overall room, it was very plain. There were a few pictures tacked to the white walls, a large chalkboard for specials, and a separate counter where I could see several pies in the display case. One of those places where more attention is spent on the food than the decoration.

Bethany came and set down my drink, along with a straw, and asked me, "What can I get you?"

"I'll have a ham-and-cheese toasty and potato-and-leek soup, please."

"That's easy enough, anything else?"

"Maybe dessert, I'll see how full I am. I noticed the cherry pie up there. It looks delicious."

Her eyes widened, "It is. All the pies are good, but I have to admit cherry is my favorite." She looked around the café and then leaned in and whispered, "Fiona mentioned that Margery put in an offer for the bookstore." She shuddered. "Her owning any business, let alone the bookstore, is frightening."

"Frightening is an apt description. Mrs. Riley mentioned she's the only one who has made an offer, but it doesn't sound as if it's going to happen, so I don't think you have to worry about it."

"Fiona mentioned you used to work there. Maybe you should buy it."

I laughed and then thought about it. "Maybe. It's something to think about."

"Well, as long as Margery doesn't get it, I'll be happy. Someone needs to get rid of her. Maybe we can take up a collection and hire a hitman. What do you think?" She winked.

"I would donate," I answered with a smile.

"I'll go put in your order and be back soon."

After lunch, I decided a walk was in order to work off the scrumptious piece of pie, so I made my way down to McGillicuddy's Cove. The tide was out, a few boats sitting lopsided in the sand. On both sides of the cove were cliffs, the Dooley Lighthouse on one point, and the remains of a tower on the other. Both looking out to sea toward New York. There was a family of four sitting on a blanket having a picnic. I smiled as the mum ran after the toddler determined to go into the water. I didn't have to test it to know it was cold. The water didn't warm up here until at least July. I took a seat on a wooden bench that needed another coat of paint and took a deep breath. The seagulls were flying above, diving for their lunch, squawking to their friends. It was so peaceful.

A man and woman arguing interrupted my tranquility. I tried to ignore them, but their raised voices kept coming closer. I recognized the one voice—who else but the bane of my existence these past few days—none other than Margery Denton. I swear the woman was stalking me. I didn't recognize the man's voice, but at least it wasn't Dillon's. I wanted so badly to turn around and see who it was but didn't want to be blatantly eavesdropping. Although I don't know why it would be since they were arguing in a public place.

The wind had picked up a little, so I could only hear bits of the conversation, a few words here and there, the rest lost in the breeze. The words guilt, wife, and kill came across crystal clear, though. If I was keeping a list of who wanted to harm Margery, I would have another person to add.

Not long after the two voices disappeared, I received a text from Aiden asking for my help, so I made way back to the pub. The afternoon and evening flew by quickly, only stopping for a quick dinner and to ask Aiden to call Dad to make sure he didn't need his car.

The festival seemed to be a hit, and I didn't return back to the house until midnight. I parked the car in the circle drive and made my way upstairs, showered, and fell into bed.

#

It was eleven o'clock before I woke up on Saturday morning. I quickly got up and took a shower.

Since we had guests, I dressed more to my mum's liking, slipping on a dress I'd picked up at the boutique. This one had three-quarter-length sleeves, solid navy blue on the top, and the bottom was navy blue with yellow polka dots and flared out at the waist. I added my blue pumps and made my way downstairs, where I found Mum in the sitting room with several other women, only one I didn't recognize. The three I did were Grandmum, Aunt

Agatha, and Mum's oldest friend, Jayne Webster. My eyes fell on the teapot, and I headed it for it.

"Good morning, everyone. Sorry I slept so late. I guess the jet lag caught up with me." I gave both Grams and Aunt Agatha a kiss and then sat on the arm of the couch next to Mum.

"Where's Doreen?" I took a sip of my tea.

"I've sent her out on some errands. She should be back soon. I don't know what's taking her so long. That stupid girl probably got lost." I could hear a gasp from someone in the room, but not quick enough to tell who it was.

"Agatha, you know that's not a very nice thing to say," Gram said. "That girl has been faithful to you for years when she could have gone to university and done something with her life rather than take care of a batty old woman."

I realized my mouth was hanging open, so I quickly took a sip of tea to hide my smile. Go, Gram!

Aunt Agatha's lips were tight, but wisely, she didn't respond. She was on the short side, her hair gray and in pin curls. What is it about older ladies and pin curls? She could be Mrs. Riley's twin. The flowered dress she wore was black with some sort of a flower pattern, but the rolls of um, extra weight, hid them from my view. My attention was diverted by Mum.

"Molly, I'd like to introduce you to Bryn Cooper. Her husband, Rob, was a school chum of your dad's." Bryn had what looked like a permanent smile on her face. I'm not sure if she was always happy, or if there had been some plastic surgery in her past. She had to be at least twenty years younger than her husband, dressed in a bright yellow sleeveless dress well fit to her slender figure. Her short blonde hair was curled to perfection, and she wore a set of shiny pearls around her neck.

I smiled back at her, and Mum moved to the last lady in the group who was sitting beside her. She placed her hand onto the lady's arm as she said, "You remember Jayne Webster, don't you?" One of my closest friends who graciously took some time off from her busy life as a judge to join us for a long weekend."

I went over and placed my arms around her neck from behind. "How have you been?" She patted my arms with her hand. Jayne had been in and out of our lives growing up. Being a judge was busy enough, but she was a judge who lived two hours south, so it wasn't always easy to get away. Usually, the parents would go to Cork and visit, and although she was also one of my favorite people, I hadn't taken the time out of my busy life to join them.

"I've been wonderful. We need to find time to catch up later," she whispered.

I let go of Jayne, and Mum said, "Sit down dear and have a cup of tea."

Jayne moved over so I could sit down between them. I refilled my cup, added the required sugar, and stirring it as I sat back.

"So where are all the men? Am I to assume Dad swept them all off for a round of golf?" I smiled as I eyed a pastry sitting on the tea tray. Dare I?

"Yes, Robby just loves to golf," Bryn answered with a giggle. "They won't be back for hours!"

"So, your mum tells us you've just returned from America. Where were you living?" Jayne asked.

"Michigan. I went to visit some cousins several years ago, fell in love, and ended up staying." I said, ready for the next question I knew was coming.

"What made you move back? Is your husband with you?" Asked Bryn. She looked around the room like I was hiding him in a closet.

"No. We're in the process of a divorce, so I moved back to be with my family."

I put my arm around Mum and squeezed. "And I'm thrilled to be back."

Mum laid her hand on my knee and said, "The feeling is mutual. I missed my girl."

"So, what do you ladies have planned for the rest of the day?" I asked, hoping it didn't involve me.

Mum spoke up, "I thought we'd take a spin around the gardens first, and then if you'd like," she looked at each of the ladies directly, including Jayne, looking around me, "we can run into the village and visit the festival."

Bryn and Jayne both said it sounded lovely, but Grandmum and Aunt Agatha declined, stating that was too much walking for their old bones, but they would enjoy a pleasant stroll in the garden.

A few minutes later, we walked onto the patio, where Mum was pointing out the newest additions to the garden. "I'm thrilled to see the fountain is working. We were having some issues with it leaking, so I'm excited they were able to fix it in time. Isn't it lovely?"

The fountain was spewing water, flowing from one tier to another, and then down to its base. It gleamed in the sunlight. Something nagged at my brain as we passed the hedges, but before it could surface, Mum explained the history of the gardens and named all the fresh flowers. It impressed me that she could remember them all, including their names in Latin.

I tuned her out, just enjoying the sunshine and blue skies. I stopped to smell some roses, breathing the sweet aroma in deeply before catching up with the others.

The tour lasted about thirty minutes, at which point we headed into town to check out the festival. We stopped by the pub, so Mum could introduce her friends to Aiden and Dillon, who talked us into staying for lunch.

Tourists and locals alike filled High Street, but we all enjoyed the afternoon. The arts and crafts portion of the festival wasn't open yesterday, so I enjoyed walking the aisles and looking at all the wares, Jayne right next to me, Mum and Bryn walking ahead of us.

"So, how's your job going? It must be fascinating." I said as I took her arm.

"It can be. It can also be heartbreaking. The young people who come through with drug charges, theft, even murder—their entire lives ruined." She shook her head as we walked.

"Still living in the same place?" I remembered a modest house in a modest neighborhood the last time I'd visited, but that was a long time ago.

"I think we've moved since you were there last. We're still in Cork City, but we moved closer to town."

"How is Jack's business? Still a solicitor, I assume?"

"Yes, and he loves it! I think that's why he and your dad get along so well. That and their mutual love of golf." She smiled.

"How long have you been married?" We had exited the arts and crafts area and were walking past the bakery as I asked, the smell of cinnamon hitting our noses as the door opened.

"Thirty years this fall," she answered.

"Wow, that's incredible! My marriage didn't even last five years." Once again, feeling that giant squid on my back.

"Well, I won't say it's all been wonderful. We've had our problems like any other couple."

"Yes, but I'm sure he probably hasn't cheated on you with the neighbor's nanny," I replied.

"No, it was one of his clients, actually," she said.

I stopped, laying my hand on her arm. "I'm so sorry. I didn't mean to—"

She smiled as she patted my hand. "Don't worry about it. It was a few years ago, and we've gotten past it."

"You're lucky. For me, the affair was the catalyst that made me realize what we had wasn't working. The more I thought about it, I'm not sure I even loved him. Well, I think I did at first, but then it all fell apart, and we were holding on to each other out of habit."

"That can happen," she said, "but you're still young. You've plenty of time."

I wasn't so sure. "How are your children doing?"

She brought me up-to-date on her three children, and the four grandchildren who were the light of her life.

"Do you plan on retiring soon, then?" I asked.

She shrugged. "Maybe. I love my job, well, most of the time, anyway, so maybe in a few years."

We walked through town, stopping to watch the three-legged race. I was standing next to Jayne when she took a sharp intake of breath. I looked at her, and she was looking across the field. I followed her gaze, but there were too many people to know who caused the reaction.

The rest of the afternoon flew by, and we decided it was time to head back and get some rest before the gala. We walked into the house, and Mrs. Jones welcomed us at the front door.

"There you are, Mrs. Quinn. The caterers are here, and they're trying to take over my kitchen. What are they doing here so early?"

Mum looked at her watch, which made me look at mine. It was four o'clock; the gala started at seven.

She looked at us and said, "I hope you all had an enjoyable time, but it looks like I'm needed in the kitchen."

Bryn and Jayne said they understood, and Mum disappeared just as the library doors opened, and Dad appeared.

"I thought I heard voices out here. Did you ladies have a pleasant time?" Dad looked a little red from the sun, but he was smiling and had a drink in his hand. I could see some men behind him, most I didn't recognize.

Bryn stopped going upstairs when she saw Dad, moving behind him and into the library. "Oh, Robby, I had such a marvelous time! Wait until you see what I bought."

Jayne answered Dad. "We did, Joseph. Thank you. Did you have an enjoyable time golfing?"

"Yes, it was a beautiful day for golf. Your husband beat me as usual, the scoundrel." He was smiling, so I don't think he minded too much. Jayne laughed. "You must not spend as much time on the golf course as he does."

"I heard that darling," said a tall man who came up behind Dad, reaching out and giving Jayne a kiss on the cheek.

I could see the adoration in his eyes for his wife. I looked at her, and she was looking at him with love in her eyes.

"Well, you golf an awful lot, dear," she said.

He nodded, "Yes, I do. But the season is so short. One must enjoy it when one can," he said, then turned to me. "Molly, you look wonderful." He took my hands and kissed my cheek. "It's been too long."

Jack was in his sixties, dressed in a dark-green polo shirt and khakis, his tanned face smiling, showing straight, white teeth. He must have recently showered, as his dark brown hair was wet, and he smelled quite nice. There was a touch of gray on the sides and a scar above his right eye. It somehow only added to his handsomeness.

He let go, and I said, "It has been a while, hasn't it? I spent a lovely time catching up with Jayne. You're a very lucky man."

"Don't I know it. I don't know what I'd do without her," his eyes shining.

Dad patted Jack on the back and said, "Let's have another drink, shall we? Ladies, would you like to join us?" He looked at Jayne and me.

We both shook our heads. "No, thank you, Dad. I need a shower and a nap to get ready for this evening."

"That's ditto for me. I'll see you later, darling," Jayne said to Jack.

We made our way up the steps, Jayne exiting to the right and myself down the hall to the left.

Chapter 9

I took a short nap, waking up at half-past five. The bathroom I shared with the room next door would be occupied by Fiona, but she hadn't shown up yet, so I took a long, hot bath, adding some lavender bubble bath and soaked away the cobwebs. I dried off, slathered myself with lotion before putting on my short robe, and sitting down at the vanity to do my hair and makeup.

I dried my hair and used my flat iron to straighten out the curls that resisted my effort, then started on my makeup. I looked at my reflection in the mirror. My heart-shaped face had gotten some sun that afternoon, so I just used a light powder before adding some blush, then worked on my eyes. I went for a smokey appearance tonight, ending with lining my eyes and a few coats of mascara.

I was excited about this evening and about seeing Callum again, but I couldn't help but wish it was Liam. I wonder what he was doing this evening? Had Sandy given birth yet? As much as I loved Callum, my feelings toward him were more like a sibling than a lover, and I hoped this evening would not bring up old feelings for him since I no longer felt the same.

I put on my nylons and slipped on my dress, along with my silver sandals. I took the small silver purse and added my lipstick and compact and headed to the ground floor, what American's would call a basement, to the ballroom.

The heavy doors stood open, and my heels clicked on the shiny hardwood floor as I walked in. I counted twenty-one, ten-top tables covered in white tablecloths, and in the center, a small bouquet with a number towering over them, and the salads all preset. Mini white lights were sparkling around the room, the chandeliers overhead dimmed, giving the room a fairytale atmosphere. Over to the side, a band was playing what I would call elevator music but hopefully would liven up later for dancing. The servers were dressed in black pants, white shirts, and black bow ties with short white jackets with gold buttons. I counted ten of them running around, adding the last touches before everyone arrived. I had taken off my watch and didn't bring my phone, so I wasn't sure what time it was. I stopped a server to ask, and they said it was six-forty-five. Everyone was most likely upstairs in the foyer, waiting for instructions to proceed to the ballroom. I took the opportunity while it was quiet to head to the bar where Scott, our favorite bartender from Shenanigans, was moving bottles around to his liking.

"Hey, Scott. Ready for organized chaos?" Dressed like the other wait staff, he looked very handsome with his hair slicked back and a huge smile. I couldn't help but smile back at him.

He leaned in and whispered, "Can you do me a favor?"

"If I can. What do you need?"

"Can you retie my tie? I can't seem to get it straight, no matter how hard I try."

Looking at it closer, it was a tad lopsided. "Sure." I walked behind the bar and retied it for him and stepped back to make sure it was straight.

"I think that will do nicely. You look very handsome." I said, picking up my clutch off the counter.

"Thank you. Now, what can I get you, ma'am?"

"I think I'd like a glass of white wine, please, sir."

He handed it to me, and I turned around and noticed a man walking in, dressed in black pants and a leather jacket. He looked very young and had a camera slung around his neck. His head was leaning all the way back, looking at the ceiling, spinning around with his mouth gaping. This must be Reanna's younger brother. The last time I'd seen him, he was a gangly teenager with his voice changing and was totally obnoxious. I walked over to him.

"Conor?" I asked.

He turned to look at me and said, "This is massive! These people must be crazy rich. Are you Evelyn?"

"Evelyn?" I wasn't sure who he was referring to until I realized that must be the event planner. "No, I'm Molly McGuire. Don't you remember me? I'm a friend of Reanna's."

He leered at me, gazing up and down. "Well, you're not the hot one, so you must be the clumsy one. Yeah, I remember you."

And…he's still obnoxious. "Yes, well. I just thought I'd welcome you. Have fun taking pictures."

"Do you think it would be okay to take pictures of the garden before everyone gets here?"

He was already walking toward the door as he asked, fiddling with his camera, so I didn't even bother to answer, I just walked away, shaking my head.

I was wondering what table they assigned me to when a teenage girl came up and said, "It doesn't look like you have one of these," and shoved a folded piece of paper in my hand. On the front, in fancy writing, it said, "Welcome to Dooley's Charity Gala" with the date and time listed. I opened it, and not only did it have the short agenda for the evening, but had listed each person by last name along with their seat number. I glanced down at my name to see I was assigned to table twelve. I double-checked Callum's name to make sure we were at the same table and then glanced to see who else had been assigned there. I was relieved to see Reanna and Dr. Fuller, as well as Jayne and Jack Webster, along with Calum's parents and Ciara's parents.

I was smiling as I heard Mum's voice, "There you are! Can you come help us greet guests, dear?" Before I could answer, she grabbed my hand and pulled me out of the ballroom, up the stairs, through the house to the crowded foyer. Higgins was at the front door, taking tickets and announcing who was entering. He placed the tickets into a gold box near his elbow attached to a tall, thin stand before moving on to the next guests.

A woman in a long black dress was standing on the stairs with a microphone in her hand. After a short welcome, she requested everyone head to the ballroom and to make sure they received the agenda for the evening, as it would have their table assignments included.

Mum stopped and said, "I think you'd be better off back in the ballroom to guide people to their tables. They will never read the agenda, but Evelyn insisted we have it."

I was about to turn around when I saw Callum come through the doorway, looking very dapper in his black tuxedo. He was saved from being mistaken as a server, as his bow tie was red with white polka dots. I loved it. His brown hair was slicked back, and his eyes were shining as he found me in the crowd.

He walked up and gave me a kiss on the cheek. "You look stunning, Molly."

"You don't look too bad yourself," I answered, taking his hand. "Come on. We're on little lost sheep duty."

"What?" he said as he followed me into the ballroom. At the door, I held my hand out to one of the young ladies, and she handed me another agenda, which I then handed to Callum.

"It's kind of like directing traffic. Just guide everyone to their tables. We're at table twelve." I kissed him on the cheek and headed to the other side of the room at the other entryway and did my best to make sure everyone got to the correct table.

By five minutes past seven, most of the guests had taken their seats when a large squawk from the microphone caught everyone's attention as Mum and Dad made their welcoming remarks.

"I'd like to welcome everyone to the gala tonight. As you know, this is for a very good cause, especially since we don't want to be sitting in church one of these days and have the roof fall onto our heads." Everyone laughed appropriately, and Dad continued. "St. Mary's is one of the oldest Catholic churches in Ireland, and it's a beautiful one at that. It warms my heart that everyone here has donated to the cause. So, without further ado, I'd like to introduce Dad Finn O'Leary, St. Mary's favorite priest." I noticed Conor taking pictures of my parents from the side of the small stage. I wondered if I'd be able to get a copy.

Everyone clapped as Dad Kearney came up and gave Mum a kiss on her cheek and shook Dad's hand, taking the microphone from him.

"What Joseph didn't say was I'm the only priest at St. Mary's, so I'm everyone's favorite by default." He smiled as everyone chuckled.

Just then, I heard a large gasp from Jayne who was sitting next to me. She leaned over to me and said, "What on earth is she doing here?" She cocked her head toward a table in front of us where I could see Margery Denton, her enormous mouth brandishing a smile, sit down next to Dillon. "Oh, her? She's Dillon's date. Well, he's trying to break up with her, but she won't go away. Do you know her?"

"Unfortunately, yes," she whispered back. I looked back at Margery. She had sat down next to Dillon, but was half out of the seat, her arms around him, smiling up to him. Dillon, however, looked like he was on the way to the dentist to get a tooth pulled. If she's trying to win him over, blatant public displays of affection aren't the way to go about it. I watched as he pulled her arms from around his neck and pushed her back in her chair. I looked back at Jayne. She'd plastered on a smile as Jack put his arm around her and held her close, even giving her head a kiss. I couldn't help but wonder how on earth Jayne could know Margery. Everyone started clapping, which pulled me out of my reverie as Dad Kearney asked everyone to bow their heads as he said a prayer, and then the staff began serving dinner.

Bethany was our server, and I gave her a welcome smile as I whispered, "How is everything going?" She smiled back and said, "So far, everything's going according to plan." I was thankful to hear that for Mum's sake. "There seems to be a lot of servers here tonight. That's nice, isn't it?"

She nodded. "Unfortunately, I have the table where Margery is sitting. Do you think it would be okay if I spit in her food?" She grinned at me, which I hope meant she was joking. Colin was walking around, taking pictures of each table, asking them all to smile. At least he had the good judgment not to take photos while their mouths were full. I looked over at Reanna, who was watching him, a huge grin on her face. Her eyes met mine, and she nodded toward Colin, her pride in him showing on her face, and said, "That's my brother!" I just smiled at her and nodded. How could she not realize he was still an obnoxious prat?

The dinner was delicious, offering salmon in a white sauce, along with a small steak, medium well, with a mushroom sauce on top, accompanied by asparagus and a small baked potato. There was a choice of lemon meringue, cherry, or apple pie for dessert. I chose lemon, and Callum chose apple. The wine flowed, and everyone seemed to have a marvelous time. Even Jayne had relaxed some, the smile reaching her eyes as the evening progressed.

It was a wonderful thing. There was dancing afterward, or I would have just rolled myself upstairs and gone to bed as I'd eaten not only my piece of pie but Jayne's too.

The band started playing livelier music, and Callum asked me to dance, so I took his hand as we walked to the dance floor.

"Did I mention that you look lovely, Molly Quinn?" he said, smiling down at me.

His use of my maiden name made me think back when we were young and stupid. Those were the days.

"Yes, but a lady never tires of hearing compliments," I answered with a grin.

"I think you've had too much wine. Your cheeks are all red," he whispered into my ear.

"Probably, but I don't care tonight," I answered as he twirled me around, and a flash went off in our faces. Conor with his camera—again.

We finished our dance and were walking back to the table when we heard raised voices. Callum and I both turned toward them to see Dillon and Margery arguing over in the corner. She was clinging to his arm, their faces both red, and I swear I could see Dillon's nostrils flaring. We both headed that way.

"I am not leaving! You invited me, and I'm staying," Margery said as Dillon shook his arm from her grasp.

"If you want to stay, then stay, but we're not longer a couple, so stay the hell away from me!" Dillon said as he stalked away.

"Dillon, are you okay?" I asked, trying to take his arm. He shook off my hand and continued walking.

I turned toward Margery, giving her a glare to make my mum proud. I smelled something rancid as we walked closer. It took me a minute to realize it was her perfume. "Maybe you should leave," I said, trying to remain civil. Why did this woman have to ruin everything?

She looked me up and down and said, "So, it was you who stole my dress!" She looked at Callum, her arms crossed in front of her, and said, "I'd like to report a robbery. Arrest her sergeant."

I rolled my eyes, "You are such a drama queen! I didn't steal the dress. You never paid for it. I did. And I strongly suggest you leave before I have the sergeant escort you out."

She stomped her foot, glaring at both of us. The black dress she had on was a halter style, the back open, and the front was barely covering her breasts. If she stomped much more, one of those babies might pop right out.

"Margery, come on. I'll walk you out." He took her arm and said to me, "I'll be right back."

Since that was taken care of, I looked around for Dillon. Spotting him in line at the bar, I walked over and asked, "Hey, are you okay?" His hair looked like he'd run his fingers through it a few dozen times, and the ends of his bow tie were loose around his neck.

"I'm fine. Is she gone?" he asked.

"Callum walked her out." He still looked a little pink, but he was calmer now.

He rubbed his face with his hand. "I hope she's gone for good because I can't take much more of her." The queue cleared just then, and Dillon ordered a beer.

"Scott, can you make that two beers and a white wine, please?" I asked.

Dillon raised his eyebrows.

"One is for Callum." Scott set the drinks on the bar, and I grabbed the beer, handing one to Dillon, then grabbed my glass of wine.

"What's going on with you two, anyway?" He took a long sip.

"We're just friends like we have been since we were twelve." I sipped my wine, savoring the sweetness, and then looked at Dillon, "You going to be okay, big brother?"

He smiled as he kissed me on the cheek. "I'm going to get plastered and then crawl upstairs to bed. Go enjoy yourself."

I watched as he walked away, glancing through the crowd to see if Callum had returned.

Instead, I found Fiona, who exclaimed, "There you are! Where have you been? I haven't seen you all night." She gave me a hug. "You look fabulous." She looked me up and down, so I did a little spin for her. "Is that beer for me?" she asked, "Or are you looking to get pissed tonight?"

"No, I'm leaving that to Dillon," I handed her the beer. "It was for Callum, but it's yours now." I looked at her dress and said, "That burgundy color looks fabulous on you." The dress was sleeveless, the high neck decorated with silver beading. She twirled, and I could see it was backless, flaring out into pleats from her tiny waist to the floor.

"I love it too. I didn't think I would like the color, but I do." She looked around, "Where is Callum?"

"He's escorting Margery out. She was making a scene with Dillon," I said as I took a sip of my wine.

"Where's your date this evening?" I asked.

"I came solo. I had asked a friend from work to be my date, but he woke up with the sniffles, so stayed at home to recover."

I spotted Conor taking pictures of the crowd, and I grabbed Fiona's arm. "Come on. I want to get a picture of the two of us." We walked over to where he was standing, his camera pointed up, taking pictures of the chandeliers. "Hey Conor, can you take a picture of me and Fiona?" I asked.

He turned toward us, his face darkening when he saw Fiona. "Oh, it's you."

They stared at each other for a few seconds before Fiona asked, "You kept up with the photography. I'm glad. You're really good at it."

"Yes. Someone once told me I needed to grow up and decide what I wanted to do. I've finally found my calling." He looked around. "Stand over here where the lighting is better," he said, walking over to another part of the room.

I was just about to ask Fiona what that was all about when Callum found us, so we asked Colin to take a few more, then other people saw what we were doing, and Conor started taking pictures of all kinds of group photos, even the catering staff.

"Will we be able to order some of these prints?" I asked when I could get his attention again.

"I'll have them to your mum in a couple of days. She'll mail you a link to my website, and you can order them from there."

"Great, thank you," I said as we walked away.

"Fiona, what was that all about?"

"I don't want to talk about it. Come on, let's dance!"

The three of us hit the dance floor, and it was three or four dances later when the band played a slow one. Callum wanted to stay on the dance floor, but I shook my head. "I need a drink." We made our way back to the table where Jayne was sitting by herself, looking upset.

"Where's Jack?" I asked.

"The restroom. He should be back momentarily. I'm just going to finish my drink, and then we're headed upstairs. It's been a lovely party." She stood up and opened her arms to Fiona, who stepped right in. "Fiona, it's so good to see you again. How did your mum end up with two beautiful daughters? I missed out only having boys."

"Molly, and I think it's because she birthed twin boys first. We're the prize." She laughed.

"Jayne, I'd like you to meet a good friend of the family. This is Callum Murphy."

They exchanged greetings, and she picked up her clutch from the table. "I'm knackered and ready for bed. Oh, here's Jack. I think I'll go say goodnight to your parents and head upstairs."

I kissed her cheek and said, "Have a good night's sleep."

"Thank you, dear. I plan to." She waved as she walked away, meeting Jack halfway across the floor.

I looked around the room. "Looks like most people have left," I said. The crowd has thinned out, but people were still milling around—mostly the younger generation. "What time is it, anyway?"

Callum looked at his watch. "It's about twelve-fifty."

I glanced around the room. The catering staff was cleaning up, stripping off the table cloths and putting them in a huge laundry bag. Once they were stripped, two other waiters came and collapsed them, adding them to a large cart that would then be rolled out to their truck.

"Anyone exciting at your table?" I asked Fiona.

"It was a decent crowd. I got to meet Reanna's parents, and Aiden and Ciara were there."

Unfortunately, Aunt Agnes and Doreen were there too. The entire table had to hear how poor Doreen was practically left at the altar after they found out the fiancé had a girlfriend on the side. I felt so bad for her. She was almost in tears! Right after dinner, she said she didn't feel well and escaped, the poor girl."

I gasped. "She told the complete story to a table full of mostly strangers? That's horrible!"

"I thought so too, but Aunt Agnes never thinks about someone's feelings. Unfortunately, after Doreen left, she talked my ear off. She finally left when she spotted some friend of hers, and I was able to escape."

Callum looked at us both and said, "How about we all go take a walk in the garden?"

The ballroom was on the ground floor with a walkout, so we headed toward the sliding glass door and walked out to the crisp evening air. I took a deep breath and sighed. A combination of sea air and fragrant blooms, how lovely.

The three of us walked up the few steps to the upper patio that ran the total length of the back of the house. I walked out into the yard and turned around, taking a look at the back of the house. There were three floors, two and a half of which you could see from the back. The ground floor comprised the ballroom, the first floor comprised the living spaces, including the kitchen, and the third floor comprised the bedrooms, with a wrap-around balcony. I closed my eyes and said a quick prayer thankful I was home where I belonged.

Fiona brought me back to reality, "It's a beautiful night, isn't it?" She pulled my arm, and we started walking toward the garden.

I looked up at the night sky, trying to find some stars, but the moon was full tonight, so you couldn't see many at all. "It is! We couldn't have asked for a better weekend for this celebration. I kept imagining we'd be traipsing through rain and mud this weekend. I'm glad the weather cooperated."

"I'm glad you're enjoying it because it's supposed to rain for the next three days," Callum said, laughing.

"It figures! I didn't really miss the rain while I was away. Michigan has its fair share, but not as much as Ireland gets." We walked along the sidewalk next to the hedges, enjoying the cool evening.

"It's not nearly as green there either, if I remember correctly," Fiona said as we followed the walkway into the inner garden.

"Not like here. Plus, Michigan winters are ten times worse. I'd never seen so much snow in my life as I saw there!"

Callum was on one side of me, Fiona, the other. "I haven't been here in a long time. When did you add the lights?"

Since I didn't know, I looked at Fiona.

"Mum added them this spring. I'm not sure why, though, considering very few people wander these gardens at night. Hey, look at the fountain. It's working!"

"Yes, there were people here fixing it yesterday." As we walked toward it, I could hear a symphony of trickling water, crickets serenading, and frogs chirping, all very soothing.

"What is that?" Fiona asked, pointing at the fountain.

I followed her finger and saw a black shape laying on the fountain. "I wonder if someone drank too much and fell? I hope they're okay."

"Stay here," Callum said as he moved closer. Neither of us obeyed, following close behind him.

The black shape was a person all right, but they weren't drunk. The face was pale, the eyes wide open, water cascading down the body, and I gasped when I saw who it was.

Chapter 10

"It's Margery," he said. "I need to call this in."

"Oh, my God," Fiona said as Callum pulled out his phone and walked away to make the call. She grabbed my hand. "Let's get out of here." She was pulling on my arm, but I shook it off.

"Wait a minute, I want a closer look."

"Why on earth would you want to look any closer? I will have nightmares for months!" She turned her face away from the fountain. "Ow!"

I turned around, and she was rubbing her foot. "Why do you have your shoes off? Are you okay?"

"Yes, I just stepped on a rock," she said, bending down and picking it up.

"You can go. I'll be fine." I glanced again at the corpse. "I've never seen a dead body before. After all the mysteries I've read and seen on the telly, I've always wondered what one would look like." I looked at my sister, her eyes wide, and her face pale.

"Look, why don't you go turn off the fountain? I think the nozzle is in on the bedroom side of the house. The water could wash away evidence."

She nodded and walked away.

I looked at Margery. Her head, torso, and part of her legs were in the fountain, drenched by the water. The rest of her legs were over the base, but not quite touching the ground. I looked at the water; it was running clear. Why was there no blood? I would think she was playing a trick on us if it weren't for the knife sticking out of her chest.

Callum came up behind me. "Come on, Molly. I need to secure the scene. My boss and a detective are on their way."

"She almost looks like she's asleep."

"Her eyes are open," Callum said.

I looked up at him, "Well, she'd look like she was asleep if she slept with her eyes open then. Maybe because her mouth is closed," I looked at Callum. "I'm sorry." I slapped my hand over my mouth.

Callum looked at me and said, "You're enjoying this, aren't you?"

"No, of course not!" I said. He raised his eyebrows at me, so I said, "Well, not exactly enjoying it. I've always wondered how I would react if I ever saw a dead body."

"She was my ex-wife for goodness sake, Molly!"

My stomach sank. How could I be so callous? "I'm so sorry! I didn't even think of that." I laid my hand on his sleeve. "Are you okay?"

He rubbed his hand over his face and then the back of his neck. "I guess. Don't tell anyone, but this is the first dead body I've seen too, outside of an autopsy I had to attend at school. It being Margery doesn't make it any easier."

The light wasn't the greatest, but I could see he was a little green. "Maybe you should go inside, and I'll secure the scene," I said, trying not to smile.

He shook his head, "I'll be fine. Where's Fiona?" he asked.

Just then, the water in the fountain stopped. I looked at him and said, "I asked her to turn off the water in case the water was washing away any evidence."

He groaned. "Damn, I should have thought of that."

"You would have. I just thought of it first. How about I go wait for the police, and I'll send them back as soon as they arrive?"

"Someone needs to tell your parents. Can Fiona do that?" he asked.

"I don't know if she's in any shape to do anything, but if she can't, I will."

He kissed me on the lips and said, "Thanks, Molly."

I gave him a smile and turned around and walked toward the house. Fiona was on her way back, but I turned her around to walk with me.

"Are you okay, Fi?" I asked.

"No, I'm not feeling too well."

"Maybe you should go to your room and lay down."

She took a few deep breaths and placed her hand on her stomach, "I think I'll be fine, but one of us needs to tell Mum and Dad."

"By one of us, you mean me?"

"Well, you are the oldest sibling here," I could see her face clearer now that we were closer to the house, and she tried to smile, but it came out more like a grimace.

"Fine, do you have any idea where they are?" I asked.

"N-no, but I can help you find them," she said, rubbing her arms.

"Fi, you're shivering. Look, why don't you grab a sweater and I'll find them, then you can wait for the police and take them to where Callum is, okay?"

She nodded, and we both went our separate ways.

I tried the ballroom first, but only catering staff remained. I noticed Conor still taking pictures, this time of the staff, as they cleaned up. He was thorough, that's for sure. I was glad he didn't know about Margery, or he'd be outside taking pictures there. Out of habit, I looked at my bare arm and grimaced. Then, I spotted Bethany.

"Bethany, can you tell me what time it is?" She continued wiping the already clear table as if in a daze.

"Bethany?" I walked up to her and touched her arm. She jumped and turned to look at me.

"Sorry, Molly. I was in my own little world." Her eyes narrowed. "Are you okay?"

"Just tired. Can you tell me what time it is?"

She looked at her wrist and said, "It's just one o'clock."

"Have you seen my parents?"

"Your parents?" She shook her head. "The last I saw them, they were closing down the bar. Maybe they're seeing someone out?"

"Maybe. Thank you."

I ran back up the stairs to the front door, but no sign of them or the butler. There were a few guests on their way out, but they hadn't seen them either. I took the stairs to the second floor, turning to the left and running down the hall to where my parents' room was, and knocked.

Dad answered, still dressed, but had taken off his tie.

"Molly, what's wrong?" he asked.

Mum was sitting on the bed, taking off her jewelry. I looked at him and said, "May I come in?"

He opened the door wider and motioned me in.

Mum took one look at my face and popped off the bed. "What's wrong, Molly? Did something happen? You're as white as a sheet."

Somewhere between the ballroom and the bedroom, it all sunk in. I looked at both of them, and Mum said, "Sit down, dear, before you fall down." She directed me to a chair, and I sat.

"Joseph, get her a drink of water."

I looked up at them. "I don't need one. There's been a murder."

They both looked at each other, and Mum said, "Nonsense, dear. There hasn't been a murder. You watch too much telly."

Dad asked, "How much have you had to drink?"

"Not enough," I said as I stood up and paced. "It's Margery, she's dead—in the fountain—stabbed." I stopped and looked at them both. "Callum called it in. His boss and a detective are on their way. They'll want to talk to all of us."

"The police? What are you talking about? It's after one o'clock in the morning!"

I took a deep breath. "Mum, I know, but I don't think we should leave her marinating in the fountain all night, do you?" I asked.

"That was uncalled for, young lady!" she said. She looked at Dad and then down at her evening dress. It was black but much more elegant than Margery's had been. Mum's had short, capped sleeves and a round neck, then at the waist, it flared out a little, but wasn't conducive to being questioned by the police.

"You might want to change your clothes, Mum," I said. "I need to let Dillon and Aiden know."

Her mum shook her head. "Dillon is already asleep, and Aiden and Ciara decided not to spend the night. They wanted to get home to the kids."

I nodded and then dashed out the door and back downstairs.

I stopped at the front door, and Fiona wasn't anywhere, so I looked outside and spotted a Garda car and a compact sedan parked down the circle. I was just about to close the door when a bright black Miata pulled into the driveway and parked behind the police car. The detective, I assumed. A tall man opened the car door, unfolded himself, and stood up, looking out toward the yard. All I could see was his broad shoulders and that his hair was dark. He turned around, and I couldn't believe my eyes.

"Liam?"

"Molly?"

"What are you doing here?" I asked. The blue jeans he wore showed off his muscular thighs. He wore a navy-blue blazer with a white-collared shirt underneath. He had a light stubble on his chin, and those cobalt blue eyes were staring at me. Man, did he look sexy. I shoved those thoughts away. Not the time or place.

I moved from the door, so he could come in.

"I was told there was a murder at this address." He looked around the room, his eyes wide, scanning the room, taking in the large foyer, the heavy oak table in the middle with the enormous bouquet on top and the white and black tiled floor.

My voice creaked. "Uh, yes," I cleared my throat. "Yes, this way. I'll show you," I pointed down the hall. He walked next to me, and I led him through the breakfast room and out the French doors and onto the patio. I stopped, and he stood beside me.

"Do you live here?" he asked, looking at the vast estate in front of him.

I didn't look at him, just answered his question. "Yes. Well, my parents live here, and I'm living with them until I find a place of my own. It's been in the family for generations. Outrageous, isn't it?"

The fountain area was blazing with lights the police must have brought in. We started walking again and were halfway down the sidewalk when we met Fiona, who fell into my arms in tears.

Liam looked at us and said, "I think I can find my way. Why don't you take her inside?"

I nodded. I led her through the house to the sitting room and sat her down on the overstuffed couch. I opened up the French doors leading out to the patio to let in some fresh air. This room overlooked the garden, normally a lovely place to sit and admire the blooms through the floor to ceiling window, but right now, it was too much of a reminder. I left her and drew the curtains, coming back to sit next to her and put my arms around her. It brought back a pleasant memory. "This reminds me of when we were children, and you'd show up in my room during a nasty storm."

She laughed through the tears. "You never yelled at me. You just opened your arms and let me crawl into bed with you."

"That's what big sisters are for." I kissed her head.

"Was that Liam I saw outside?"

"It was. Turns out, he's a detective." Just then, I heard footsteps, so I glanced at the door. It was our parents.

"Fiona, my dear! Are you okay?" Mum had changed into a pink sweater and gray pants and sat down on the other side of Fiona, who sat up quickly and fell into Mum's arms. I handed her a tissue from the box on the end table. Her eyes were red and puffy, and her mascara was running down her cheeks. I stood up and walked toward Dad. I took his arm and led him outside to the patio.

His eyes zeroed in on the brightly lit fountain before turning to me to ask, "Explain again what happened."

I went over the story, rewinding it like a movie, only leaving out that I knew the detective. Callum walked up to us as I finished. He put his hand on my arm and said, "Are you okay? You look a little pale." He took his jacket off and laid it over my shoulders.

I pulled it closer. "Thanks." I nodded toward the fountain. "What's going on?"

"The coroner has arrived. They're taking pictures now; they'll see what evidence they can find. They'll need to talk to whoever is still here." He rubbed the back of his neck. "I didn't even think about telling people they couldn't leave."

"When I went to the ballroom to look for Mum and Dad, there weren't too many people left except for the catering staff."

Dad was standing there, his arms crossed over his chest as he questioned Callum. "So, there's no way this could have been an accident?"

Callum looked my dad straight in the eye, "No, sir. It looks like murder."

"Dad, there was a knife in her chest. That pretty much rules out an accident." I pulled the coat tighter.

"Now, Molly, there's no need to get smart."

I closed my eyes and took a deep breath. "Sorry, I don't come across bodies all that often."

"That often? Does this mean this isn't your first?" Dad asked.

I looked from one to the other. "No—I mean yes. It doesn't matter. I'll explain later."

Callum looked at me for a second longer before turning his gaze to Dad. "Mr. Quinn, would it be possible to get a copy of the guestlist?"

"I'm sure Deidre can get that for you. She's dealing with Fiona right now, though." He took my arm and said, "Let's go inside where it's warmer."

Higgins was just walking into the room as we walked in from outside. He had a tray in his arms with a pot of tea and set it on the table. "Mrs. Jones and I heard all the commotion and were told what happened. She thought everyone could use some tea."

I looked at him with a smile. "Thanks, Higgins. You and Mrs. Jones are priceless."

Higgins looked at Dad. "Anything else, sir?"

Dad shook his head. "We're all set. Thank you, and please thank Mrs. Jones." He poured a cup and handed it to me.

"Let me know if you require anything else." He turned and walked out the door.

Callum said, "I'm going to the ballroom to ask everyone still there to stay. I'll be back."

I added two teaspoons of sugar and stirred it before taking it over to Fiona, who was still in Mum's arms.

"Fi? Come on, you need to drink this. It will make you feel better."

She sat up and took a sip from the cup.

"Yuck—it has sugar in it!" She looked at me accusingly as Mum glared.

"For shock! In all the books I've read, they always add sugar to help with shock."

Mum asked, "And how is it supposed to help?"

I shrugged. "I don't know! But it seems to…in the books, anyway."

Mum glared. "This isn't one of your mystery books, Molly Colleen!"

Ooh—middle name. I took the cup back and said, "Blimey, I'll get her a fresh one without sugar." I sat that one down on the table. Dad poured another one and handed it to me, trying to hide his smile.

I handed it off to Fiona and then took a sip of the one I'd set on the table. Heaven.

We heard footsteps, then turned to watch Liam walk in the door. He was reaching in his pocket for something before stopping next to the table where Dad and I were still standing. Callum hadn't returned yet, so I did the introductions.

"Mum, Dad, this is Detective Fitzgerald." They shook hands. "Detective, this is Deidre and Joseph Quinn, my parents, and my sister, Fiona." I smiled, hoping he didn't mind my not mentioning how the three of us knew each other.

"Molly, please pour me a cup of tea—without sugar?" Mum asked.

I poured her a cup and handed it to her as Callum walked in.

Liam said, "It's nice to meet you both. I'm just sorry it's under these circumstances."

"Detective, would either you or Callum like a cup of tea?" Mum asked, throwing daggers at me. I just pasted a smile on my face, trying to unclench my teeth. It's not my fault. I don't know the correct formalities when being interviewed during a murder investigation.

"I'm good for now, ma'am." He nodded toward Mum with a smile, and then looked at Callum, "Who exactly found the body?"

Callum walked over and poured himself a cup as he said, "We all did, sir. I mean, Molly, Fiona, and myself. We'd gone for a walk in the garden when we found her."

Liam made notes in his notebook as Dad asked, "Detective, can you tell us what's going on?"

Chapter 11

Liam's lips tightened as he gazed at us, "We're just at the preliminary stages of the investigation. All I can tell you is," he looked at his notebook, "the victim, Margery Denton, is dead, found stabbed in your garden fountain." He looked at Mum. "Was she a guest tonight?"

She nodded. "She was a guest of our son, Dillon." She continued to rub Fiona's back.

"And where might he be at this time?" He poised his pen over his notebook.

Mum had gone pale, her eyes going wide, and she looked at Dad. "You can't think…"

I jumped in. "Mum, the detective needs to rule Dillon out, and to do so, he has to talk to him." I looked at Liam, "He's upstairs asleep. We'll wake him up."

Fiona had finished her tea, her head laying back on Mum's shoulder, her eyes closed.

Liam looked at Dad. "Is there someplace private I can use to conduct interviews?" His pen pointed at Callum, Fiona, and me, "starting with the three of you."

Dad nodded, "You can use the library. Either Callum or Molly can show you the way. I'll go wake up, Dillon." His eyes softened when they landed on his youngest daughter. "Detective, is there any way you can wait to speak to Fiona until tomorrow? She's taking this a little hard."

I could see his jaw clench as he nodded. "I can speak with her in the morning."

"Thank you, detective." Mum smiled at him.

Callum spoke up then. "Detective, I asked everyone still in the ballroom not to leave the premises, and Mr. Quinn agreed to give us a guestlist."

He nodded. "Excellent work, sergeant."

I added, "Callum, why don't you take him to the library, and I'll work on getting the guestlist for you."

They walked to the door, and I looked at Mum. "Is the guestlist on your laptop?"

"Yes, it's up in my sitting room. I think I'll get Fiona to bed now." She stood up with Fiona still in her arms. "Can you walk, dear?"

She was still deathly pale, but she nodded, and she and Mum walked out of the room. I stayed behind to think as I took a sip of my tea, which was barely lukewarm, adding more to warm it up.

I couldn't help but wonder who would have killed Margery. My mind scanned over the list I'd encountered since I'd been home, but who knows how many others there were. The list could be endless. I finished my tea, setting the cup on the tray before heading upstairs to my parents' room. It wasn't hard to find the database file. Looking at the report options, I chose the guestlist that included addresses and phone numbers and headed down to the library. The door was closed, so I knocked.

"Come in!"

I walked in, expecting to see Liam and Callum, but Liam was alone. I closed the door behind me.

"Where's Callum?" I asked. Liam was sitting behind the desk. I handed him the guestlist.

"He went to make sure no one left." He glanced at the list, then at me with raised eyebrows. "Three pages?"

I smiled. "That list is just those who paid for a ticket. I'm sure the actual guestlist was much longer."

He set the pages down and then looked at me, nodding toward the chair, and said, "Please, sit down." He sat back in his chair, glancing through the three pages and then set them down.

I took a deep breath and sat down, realizing how tired I was. I smiled as I looked at him. "Nice to see you again."

He smiled back. "It's good to see you too. I just wish the circumstances were better." He ran his hand over the back of his neck.

"Me too." I tilted my head, drinking in the sight of them.

"Your boyfriend tells me this Margery person wasn't very well-liked."

"Ha! That's an understatement, but for the record, Callum isn't my boyfriend, he's just a friend. I've known him since I was twelve. As for Margery, the list would be much shorter if we wrote down those who actually liked her." Thinking about it, I wasn't aware of anyone who did.

"How about you?" He sat up, poised to write in his little book.

"I couldn't stand her." I waited for his response.

He smiled.

"Why are you smiling?"

"I rarely have someone admit they hated the victim. They're afraid they'll be a suspect." He looked at me with those penetrating eyes.

I met his gaze, "I know enough about criminology to realize I'm a suspect." I started to count on my fingers. "One, I was one of those who found the body, two, I disliked her and three…"

"Three?" His eyebrows raised.

I smiled. "I'm sure there's a three, but I'm tired. I'll have to think about it."

He smiled as he took notes. "Why did you dislike her?" He looked up.

"She was the typical 'mean girl.' She loved to cause trouble."

"Such as?"

"Let's see. She got me in trouble in elementary school when she stole a bracelet and stuck it in my backpack. I almost got expelled for that one. When I was sixteen, she stole my boyfriend from me, which annoyed me at the time, but ended up being a favor as he wasn't much of one. And—"

"You don't hold a grudge or anything, do you?" He was smiling, so I couldn't help but return it.

"I was just getting started. She went from being a teenager who loved to cause trouble to an adult who loved to cause trouble. It's almost like she was miserable, so let's make everyone else feel that way."

"How well did you know her? You've only been home a few days."

"Dooley is a small village, and for some unknown reason, she hated me from a very early age, so everything between us became a competition. I joined the swim team; she joined the swim team. If I went out for the lacrosse team, so did she. If there was a boy who liked me, she did her best to intervene. I think that was a contributing factor to her and Callum ending up married."

"As in Callum Murphy?"

I nodded.

"Continue, please."

"Like I said, he and I have known each other since we were twelve. There were four of us who hung out together. However, when we got out of university, things became a little more serious between Callum and me. However, I went to America, where I met my husband. I came home, broke things off with Callum, and returned to America. I hadn't seen or spoken to him until I returned home."

"So, you were jealous?" His brow furrowed.

"Jealous? God, no. It didn't take me long to realize I loved him as a brother. I knew they'd gotten married, but I wasn't told they'd divorced until I came home."

"Anything else?" His blue eyes catching mine.

"Well, I heard she got married again to someone much older than she was who died under mysterious circumstances."

"Do you know when?"

I tried to remember if Fiona had mentioned it.

"No worries. I can find that out. Anything else?"

"She was trying to buy the local bookstore in town, but the current owner didn't like her."

"Who was that?"

I laughed. "Mrs. Beatrice Riley, who is seventy years old and wouldn't have killed her, let alone strong enough to throw her in the fountain. Besides, many others had a much stronger motive."

"Such as your brother?"

My eyes narrowed. "Dillon would never hurt anyone. True, they argued...." Crap! I didn't mean to say that.

He sat up a little straighter. "Argued?"

"He was trying to break up with her, and she wouldn't take the hint. She kept bothering him, and so they got in a small, heated argument." I held my fingers a small distance apart.

"When was this?"

"Tonight, after dinner. Callum and I intervened, and he..." Crap!

Liam sighed. "Yes?"

"Callum walked her out, and that was the last I saw of her."

He dropped his pen and sat back. "Great."

"Look, she was unstable. Anyone can tell you that. For goodness gracious, she wanted Callum to arrest me for stealing her dress!"

"Wait, you stole her dress? What dress?"

I grinned. "The dress I have on, but I didn't steal it. From what I can gather, she ordered it but never picked it up. I came in looking for a dress, and the owner showed it to me. She saw me wearing it at the gala tonight and wanted Callum to arrest me."

He didn't cover up the smile this time. "You look beautiful."

My stomach did a little flip as I smiled back and said, "Is that an appropriate way to speak to a suspect, Detective Fitzgerald?" I lifted my eyebrows.

He cleared his throat and picked up his pen. "You're right, Mrs. McGuire. We can put that on hold for now. Besides, it looks like I need to get a new sergeant assigned to this case." He leaned back into the chair and put his arms behind his head.

I sat up straighter. "Why? Because he's a suspect too?"

"Everyone's a suspect at this point." He started fiddling with his pen, and his eyebrows furrowed. I could tell he was mulling things over in his mind. Just then, there was a knock on the door.

"Come in!"

Callum walked in and sat down next to me. "Everyone is still there, but they're getting a little restless. Molly was right. Most of the people down there are the catering staff and that irritating photographer, Conor West, who is still down there taking pictures. Before we continue, though, sir, I have a confession to make." He stood up, his arms behind him, ramrod straight.

Liam sat back in his chair and said, "Something like the deceased was your ex-wife?" He looked at me and then back at Callum.

Callum cleared his throat, glanced at me quickly, and then back at Liam.

"Yes, sir," he croaked.

Liam rubbed his hand over his chin and looked at Callum.

Liam sat up straight and said, "Thank you for being straight with me, Murphy. This does, however, mean I have to take you off of the investigation."

"But, sir—"

"No, buts! You're the victim's ex-husband, and you're a suspect! I can't have you involved in this at all." He fell back into his chair.

"Yes, sir," he said and sat back down.

"How many people are we looking at in the ballroom?"

"Fifteen, sir."

Liam got on his phone and called someone. A few minutes later, there was a knock on the door.

"Come in."

Two young officers, one male, one female, walked in the door and stood next to Callum.

"I want you two to go to the ballroom and take statements from everyone who is still there. Make sure you take down everyone's name, address, and phone number. Make sure you get the same information for any staff member who worked tonight and is no longer on the premises. Once you've received the information, they're free to go, but make sure they realize we may need to question them further and not to leave town. You can complete your reports in the morning, but I want them sent to my email no later than noon. Understood?"

They both nodded, turned around, and left.

Liam looked at me and said, "Mrs. McGuire, will you excuse us for a few minutes while I speak to Sergeant Murphy?"

I stood up. "Sure. Are we done for tonight?" I felt like I had been pushing a rock uphill all day long and could hardly keep my eyes open. If my brain would just stop twirling around like a tornado, I might be able to sleep tonight.

"I know it's late, but I have just a few more questions. Can you give us twenty minutes?"

I looked at the clock on the wall. It was one forty. I nodded and walked out of the room. Dillon was pacing back and forth in the foyer. He stopped when he saw me. "I'm in trouble, aren't I?"

I sighed. "Probably. You had motive, means, and opportunity," I said, not sugar-coating it.

"I didn't do it, Molly." He brushed his hand over his face, a slight stubble showing.

"I know you didn't. The question is. Who did?" He had thrown on a pair of jeans and a tee-shirt, and he looked tired, but thankfully, not drunk.

The door opened, and Callum came out and said, "Dillon, the detective will see you now."

Dillon walked in, and Callum closed the door, coming to stand next to me.

"Not how I figured this evening would end." He took hold of my hand.

"I'm sorry you're off the case." I pulled him toward the love seat, and we both sat down. "Me too. I think I could learn a lot from that detective."

"What do you know about him?" I couldn't help but be curious about this side of him.

"Not a lot. He has an excellent reputation. He takes his time in an investigation and is not one to jump to conclusions or look for a simple way to close the case. You're in excellent hands."

"We're really suspects, aren't we?"

He nodded. "I'm probably number two on the list after Dillon. I was the last one to see her. If I was investigating this, even I would be on my suspect list."

"Yes, but you weren't gone long enough to kill her. I can attest to that. What, maybe fifteen minutes?" I tried to remember.

He turned his head to me and said, "Plenty of time to drag her out to the garden, stab her with a knife and throw her in the fountain."

I looked at him, my eyes wide. "I don't think she was thrown there; I think she fell back onto it." I got up and started to pace. "Margery is out by the fountain. Either someone asked her to meet them there, or she was out there getting some fresh air. She's looking at it. Someone comes up behind her and says her name. She turns and sees someone with a knife. She struggles with them, but they stab her anyway. She falls back into the fountain."

"Sounds plausible."

"Okay. But where is the blood? Wouldn't you have blood on your clothes?"

"I didn't notice any blood at the scene, did you?"

"No, I didn't. Isn't that strange?"

"I've read about it. It has something to do with where the knife lands in the heart."

"Okay, you're not making this very easy. Let's think about who would want her dead. I know many people disliked her, but who would want to kill her?

"I'm just thinking like the detective will. I'm a good suspect." He stood up and walked over to me. "Time for me to head home." He kissed me on the forehead. "I'll talk to you tomorrow." He smiled. "Or rather, later today."

I handed him his coat back and saw him out, closing and locking the door behind him. I leaned back on it and closed my eyes. Who would do such a thing? I took the stairs to the second floor and walked into my room and leaned against the door for a moment. God, was I tired! I didn't glance at the bed, as I was afraid to be tempted to fall down on it. Instead, I hung up my dress and put my pearl necklace back in its case before changing into a pair of jeans and a turtleneck sweater and added my watch to my wrist. Checking the time, I still had ten minutes. Time enough to go to the kitchen and make tea. I needed something to help me stay awake. I slipped on some shoes and made my way to the kitchen. Higgins was pouring boiling water into two teapots, and Mrs. Jones was making sandwiches. They were whispering to one another but stopped once I walked in.

"You two are saints! Do you mind if I take one of these to the library? The detective is holding some interviews in there."

Higgins, still dressed in his fancy butler uniform, put the teapot on a tray. "We heard what happened, Miss Molly. I'd like to offer my condolences."

"Thank you, Higgins, but to be honest, I didn't care for her much. However, she didn't deserve to die that way." I leaned against the counter as they finished what they were doing.

"We're taking the trolley out to the policemen who are working out at the fountain. We thought they might appreciate a cup of tea and some snacks," Mrs. Riley said.

"I'm sure they will. Are there many still here?" How long does it take to work a crime scene, I wonder?

Higgins added a plate to the tray. Mrs. Jones added a few sandwiches, and Higgins picked it up.

"I can take that, Higgins."

He and Mrs. Jones shared a look, then she looked at me as Higgins handed me the tray. "Just be careful, Miss. You remember what happened last time."

"I was twelve!"

"That wasn't that long ago to me, Miss."

I sighed as I turned around and walked down the hall to the library. I must admit I did walk slower than normal and made it without a mishap. However, I realized I couldn't open the door, so I glanced around for a place to set the tray. The table on the foyer was too far away, so I chose the floor. I had just set it down when the door to the library opened, hitting me in the behind and sending me flying. I landed on my shoulder and arm, miraculously missing the tea tray.

"Molly! Are you okay?"

I looked up, and Dillon was having trouble hiding his smile.

"It's not funny!"

Liam came out behind Dillon and saw me on the floor, rubbing my arm, and he too smiled. "What's going on?"

Dillon came over to me and offered his hand. "My sister's a klutz."

"I am not a klutz. I'm just gravity—"

Dillon laughed. "I know, gravity challenged. You told me."

I looked at Liam, who smiled.

"I was bringing in some tea and sandwiches when someone..." I scowled at Dillon, "opened the door."

Liam bent over and picked up the tea tray as Dillon said, "I am going back to bed." He kissed me on the cheek.

"Goodnight."

Chapter 12

Liam was still smiling as he set the tray on the desk.

I ignored him, walking in and setting the tray on the desk. I poured two cups of tea, adding sugar to mine. I looked at Liam, "How do you take it?"

"Black, please."

I handed him his tea and then went over to the wall unit, lifted the door, and pulled out a bottle of Bushmill's. I added some to both of our drinks and set the bottle back on the desk.

I nodded at the plate of sandwiches. "Help yourself to sandwiches too. I'm not sure what kind they are," I placed one on a small plate for myself.

Liam took one, and we both sat there eating. Mine was tuna. Not my favorite, but I hadn't realized how hungry I was. I lifted the guestlist I'd given Liam. "May I?"

He nodded. "I've only glanced at it. Do you have any idea how many are out of town?" He finished his first sandwich and took another one off the plate.

I took the list and started looking through it. "I printed off the list with everyone's address and phone numbers, so you'll be able to tell. There are a few of them staying here. Those who aren't may be housed with friends or relatives."

He handed me a pen. "Can you mark who those are?"

"Sure." I started looking at the list.

Liam's phone buzzed, and he looked at it, then made a note in his notebook.

"What time was dinner finished?"

I thought about it for a few seconds before answering, "Maybe around half-past eight? Nine at the latest?" I finished the last page and handed the list back to Liam, explaining my system.

"I put checkmarks next to those staying at the house and stars next to my siblings, who are here just for the night. There are six listed from out of town that I'm not sure about. My grandparents, Aunt Agatha and Mr. and Mrs. Webster, are all here. Mum may know where the others are staying." I sat back in the chair, stretching a little to stay awake.

He looked at his watch and groaned. "Any suggestions on where I can sleep tonight rather than making the drive back to Ballyquicken?"

My head snapped up, and I grinned.

He grinned back at me. "Let me rephrase that. Is there a hotel or pub that offers guest accommodations in town?"

I stopped myself from fanning my heated face, "Not at this time of night. However, you can stay here. We have plenty of room."

"Are you sure it won't be a problem?"

"Mum expected a sizeable amount of people, so I'm sure she won't mind." I placed my teacup and plate on the tray and said, "Do you have any further questions?"

Just then, Liam's phone rang. He looked at it and said, "Excuse me."

"Fitzgerald."

He listened for a minute. "Thanks, Gary. I'll be staying here at the Quinn home, so we can go over this all tomorrow when you get here." He discontinued the call and sat back in his chair.

"So, Detective Fitzgerald, are we done here?" Just then, I yawned, quickly covering my mouth. "Sorry."

He smiled, looking at me intently, "It seems like a long time since our plane ride, doesn't it?"

"It does. It's been a whirlwind week."

"If you don't mind going over everything from the time you arrived back in Ireland to the end of the gala one more time to make sure I haven't missed anything."

I went over all the events I'd witnessed or heard about since I'd been back home. He stopped me occasionally to clarify something or ask me a question.

"You don't know who the man was you heard Margery talking to in the park?"

I shook my head.

"And you're sure no one touched the knife?"

"I'm positive neither Fiona nor I did, nor I'm sure, did Callum."

He let out a deep sigh and said, "I can see why you think there are more people who may have wanted to kill her than didn't." He closed his notebook. "It's late," he looked at his watch, "or rather early. Why don't you show me where I'll be sleeping, and we'll continue this in the morning?"

I nodded, cleaning up the tea things. "Do you want me to carry that for you?" he asked.

I shook my head. "I'll take this into the kitchen and meet you at the bottom of the stairs in a few minutes."

"I'll go run out to my car and get my things and meet you there."

I picked up the tray, and he opened the door for me. I made my way carefully to the kitchen, where I dropped off the tray.

Ten minutes later, I had seen Liam to the room down the hall from mine, and I was in bed, sure I wouldn't be able to sleep with him so close. I rolled over and closed my eyes. However, it's was Liam's image that filled my head. It was Margery's, staring back at me like this was all my fault.

#

A loud crack of thunder woke me Sunday morning much earlier than I preferred. I looked at my watch, and it was eight o'clock. What little time I'd spent in bed, I'd tossed and turned, not being able to get Margery's death off my mind.

I got up, pulled out my laptop, and opened a blank document. I listed everything I knew about Margery and all the people I'd come into contact with who disliked her. Unfortunately, my name was at the top.

Molly McGuire
Callum Murphy
Beatrice Riley
Dillon Quinn
Scott the bartender
Jayne Webster

Looking at the list, the only one I could cross off for certain was myself. Like I said to Liam, I was sure Mrs. Riley had nothing to do with this. I thought back to mysteries I'd seen or read. What would they do?

I looked at my list of names. What do I know about each of these people pertaining to Margery?

Molly McGuire couldn't possibly have done it, regardless of how much she disliked the victim.

Callum Murphy married Margery five years ago. Divorced after six months. Doesn't appear to have any feelings for her at all, let alone murderous ones.

Beatrice Riley wouldn't sell the bookstore to her, didn't like her because she was a "hussy" and was an unpleasant customer.

Dillon Quinn broke up with Margery, but she wouldn't accept it. Had an argument with victim before she was killed. (What time was she killed?)

<u>Scott, the bartender,</u> wasn't fond of her, but why? Because she wouldn't leave Dillon alone, or did he date her as well at some point?

<u>Jayne Webster</u> knew Margery, but not sure how.

Looking at the list, I realized I needed more information, so I took a quick shower and got dressed in a light-blue pleated skirt and a white and blue polka-dot short-sleeved blouse. I topped it with my navy-blue cardigan, slipped into my navy-blue sandals, added enough makeup to cover the dark circles, and made my way downstairs.

I walked into the breakfast to find my parents, Aunt Agatha, and Doreen sitting around the large breakfast table. Liam hadn't yet made an appearance. I was glad to know I had time to let Mum know he'd spent the night.

The four of them were discussing the "ruckus" last night, as Aunt Agnes put it, so I guess I didn't have to worry about keeping anything a secret.

"Good morning, everyone." I smiled, as if I'd had a full night's sleep, and my body wasn't screaming for caffeine. I grabbed a cup, filled it with tea and required sugar, sitting down between Mum and Doreen. I kissed Mum on the cheek.

"Did you get any sleep last night?" Mum took a sip of her tea.

"Not much. How about you?" I lifted my cup and took a sip, wishing I liked coffee. I needed a larger jolt of caffeine than this offered.

She shook her head. "Have you seen Fiona this morning?"

"I looked in on her, but she was still sleeping. Oh, by the way, Detective Fitzgerald spent the night."

She almost dropped her teacup, looking at me, her eyes wide, "What?"

"Why are you looking like that? I gave the detective the room that Aiden didn't use. I hope that's all right."

Dad chuckled as Mum's face relaxed.

I looked at them both, "What?" I went over the words I'd said in my mind and smiled. "Sorry, I see how that sounded." Not that I would have minded.

I pushed back my chair and walked to the sideboard to get some breakfast when Liam walked in. I smiled at him. Dressed in a pair of black dress pants and a white and black striped shirt with a black tie. He didn't have a jacket on, but I figured there was probably one in the library. He walked over to Mum's chair and said, "Thank you so much for allowing me to stay last night, Mrs. Quinn."

"Think nothing of it, detective. Did you sleep well?" She turned and looked up at him.

Aunt Agatha's head turned sharply when she heard the word "detective." Doreen, however, seemed to be looking off into space.

"I did. Thank you," he said, standing behind my parents. He bent down and whispered, and then Dad nodded his head.

"Help yourself to some breakfast," Mum said, nodding to the long table set up for the buffet.

"Thank you. I will." He walked over next to me as I was filling my plate with ham, eggs, toast, and potatoes.

"Good morning, Mrs. McGuire."

"Good morning, Detective Fitzgerald." I turned to go back to my seat. Liam followed a few minutes later and set his plate down. Then, he went back for tea and sat down across from me.

Dad looked at Aunt Agnes and Doreen. "Ladies," he waited until they looked at him and then nodded toward Liam, "this is Detective Liam Fitzgerald with the Garda.

There was an…incident last night, and he'll need to speak to you at some point this morning."

Aunt Agnes pointed her fork at Liam. "It will need to be soon because I will not miss mass. I haven't missed mass in twenty-years, and I don't plan on starting now."

"What time is mass this morning?" Liam asked, looking around the table.

"Eleven," Mum answered.

"I should be able to get to you by then, Mrs.?"

"Well, Quinn, of course! I'm Joseph's aunt. His dad was my brother." Then, she motioned her toast toward Doreen. "And this is my granddaughter, Doreen."

"Yes, of course. Well, it's nice to meet you both." He looked at his watch. "I have a constable and another detective arriving shortly, and we can begin."

"Just who was this person who died anyway? Do we even know her?" Aunt Agnes asked.

Liam answered her. "A woman by the name of Margery Denton, ma'am." There was a gasp from Doreen who was sitting next to me. I glanced over. Her head was down, her glasses sliding off her nose. She was twisting her napkin with her fingers, and I swear I heard her whisper, "That horrible woman deserved it."

"Doreen, did you know Margery?" I held my teacup close to my mouth, hoping no one would notice.

She looked at me, her eyes wide. She'd gone pale and was trembling. I put my hand on hers and squeezed it. "Are you okay?" She shook her head slightly. I'd have to find her later to see if I could help.

Aunt Agatha asked, "Is she the woman I saw arguing with Dillon last night?" She took a bite of her food.

I looked at her, wondering what she'd seen. "It was more of a discussion than an argument, and Sergeant

Murphy took care of it." Just then, Fiona walked in looking pale, her eyes bloodshot and puffy, wearing a black dress with a peter pan collar. She walked to the teapot, poured herself a cup of tea, and sat down across from me.

"How are you, dear?" Mum asked.

"I'm all right. Just a slight headache." I gave her a smile and continued to eat my breakfast.

Liam left the room shortly after that, and I lasted a whole five minutes before following him. I was walking down the hall, wondering what excuse I could give for intruding when the doorbell rang. I opened the door to find a young, skinny gentleman in a Garda uniform, a name tag attached that said "MILLS." I gave him a smile as I opened the door wider. "Come in, Constable Mills."

"How did ya know who I am, ma'am?" His eyes narrowing.

I leaned into him and whispered, "Don't tell anyone, but I'm psychic."

His eyes got very wide. "Really? I won't tell a soul, ma'am. I have an Aunt Eunice who has the sight." He leaned in and whispered to me, "I think she has some fairy blood in her too. That must be how you got it. And I'll keep your secret. I'm a man of the law."

I bit my lip to keep from bursting out in laughter as he walked in and I closed the door. "Are you hear to see Detective Fitzgerald?"

His eyes widened, "You know that too? You are good." He shook his head.

"The library right here." I turned around and knocked on the door.

"Come in."

I opened the door and motioned for Constable Mills to go first. He walked up to the desk and said, "Constable

Mills reporting for duty." He stood ramrod straight, and I half expected him to salute.

Liam looked at him and said, "You're late."

I looked at my watch and noticed it was two minutes after the hour. The constable was sweating, so I said, "That was my fault, detective. We were chatting."

I hoped Liam was joking with the poor constable, but I couldn't tell. Liam looked at him up and down, "Do you know what your duties are today?"

"Yes, sir. Whatever you tell me, sir." He had relaxed slightly but was still standing straight, his arms at his sides.

"Good man. Now, I will be interviewing today. Your job is to take notes. Do you have your notebook and pen?"

Constable Mills unbuttoned his front pocket and pulled out a small, black notebook along with a pen. "Where should I sit, sir?"

"No need to call me, sir, constable."

"Yes, sir, I mean—detective," he answered. Liam looked around the room and saw a chair sitting next to a small table near the window. He nodded at it. "You can sit there," then he turned his gaze to me. His eyes softening a little, thank goodness.

"Did you remember anything else about last night?"

"Um, no, not really. I was just curious whether or not you've received the preliminary autopsy results. Was there anything surprising?"

"The autopsy's not in yet, but I don't think there will be any surprises. Why do you ask?"

"Nothing really. There just wasn't any blood, which with a knife wound, I thought that was surprising."

"Sometimes, the blood stays in the body, so there isn't much at the scene," His hands were clasped on the desk, his laptop to the side.

"It's called a cardiac tamponade."

We both looked at Constable Mills.

"A what?" I asked.

"When the blood stays in the body. It's called a cardiac tamponade. It's the accumulation of the blood in the pericardial sac. The sac that surrounds the heart. The blood fills the sac, and the heart stops beating, but there's little or no blood at the scene."

Liam and I looked at each other, then at the constable.

"How on earth would you know such a thing?" Liam asked.

Chapter 13

He shrugged. "My dad's a doctor. I read his medical books sometimes."

Liam turned back around and looked at me with raised eyebrows. I looked at the constable and said, "Thank you, Constable Mills. I guess I've learned something today."

"You're welcome, ma'am."

"Would you like any tea or water? I can have either Higgins or Mrs. Jones bring some in."

"That's kind of you. A pitcher of water and some glasses would be good. Thank you." He smiled. Can you also send your sister in?"

I nodded as I walked out of the room, smiling as I closed the door. That Constable Mills was quite a surprise. I guess what they say about not judging a book by its cover is correct.

I was still smiling when I reached the breakfast-room door, glancing in to make sure Fiona was still there. I walked up and whispered to her, "You're wanted in the library."

She slid out her chair, got up, and walked out of the room. The Coopers and Websters were now sitting at the table with my parents. I went to leave when I spotted Dillon, who was standing at the window, his hands wrapped around a teacup.

I walked over to him and laid my hand on his back and my head on his shoulder. "Did you get any sleep?"

"Not really. You?" He took a sip of his tea, still looking out the window.

"Not much." I followed his gaze. He was looking at the fountain, still turned off, and I could see police tape surrounding it. I looked up at him, "We know you didn't do it, and the police will figure that out too. What time did you go up to your room? Do you remember?"

He tilted his head. "Not exactly. After I saw you, I finished my beer, went to the bar, and asked Scott for a bottle of whiskey. I actually hadn't drunk much of it when Dad came and told me the detective wanted to see me." He turned around from the window and went and sat at the table.

"After I got back to my room, I had another drink and fell asleep."

"Who would do such a thing?" my mum asked.

"It was probably someone who saw the party and saw it as a splendid opportunity to rob someone. She was probably in the wrong place at the wrong time. We see it all the time, don't we, Joseph?" Jack said, looking toward my dad.

Dad answered, "Well, yes, it happens, and I'd like to think it was a stranger versus someone we know, but Jack, you and I both know, as does Jayne, that most of the time these types of crimes happen by people the victim knows."

"That's horrible!" my mum said. "You can't honestly think someone we know did this?" She looked at her husband with wide eyes, and then toward Jack, Jayne and me.

"Mum, Higgins put everyone's tickets into a box. Do you know where it is?" An idea was coming to mind.

Dad answered, "I put it in the library. It should be on the shelf behind the desk on the left side." He smiled.

"Why do you need it, dear?" Mum asked.

"To narrow down the suspect pool, right, Molly?" My dad asked, smiling. "Forever my Nancy Drew."

I smiled at the reference to the summer I read all of the Nancy Drew books. My parents thought it was great until I began to be suspicious of anyone in the village I'd never met before. They put a stop to it when I interrogated a gentleman I thought had been lurking around the church. It turned out it was Dad Kearney who had just been assigned to our parish.

Dad asked Dillon, "How did your talk go with the detective last night?"

He shrugged. "As well as I expected. The detective didn't come right out and accuse me, but he made it clear I'm a suspect."

"Since your dad can't represent you, if it comes to that, Dillon, I'd be glad to do so," Jack added.

Dillon lifted his head and said, "Thank you, Jack. That's nice of you. Hopefully, it won't come to that, but if it does, I'll take you up on it. How long are you here for?" He took a sip of his tea, made a face, and set it back down.

"We planned on staying a few days, but I'm sure at some point we'll be told not to leave town, so it may be a few days longer."

"Oh, goodness gracious. I really need to speak to Mrs. Jones." Mum scooted back her chair and excused herself. She scurried out of the room, a look of panic on her face. Dad and I shared a look. Regardless of the circumstances, Mum was in her element.

As Mum walked out, Fiona walked in. She was a little paler than when she left and looked at our brother. "Dillon, the detective would like to see you again." Dillon slid out his chair, took a deep breath, and stood up. "I wonder what he wants now?"

I decided now was a good time to get the box of tickets as any, so followed Dillon out. The doorbell rang, and I saw Higgins coming out of the sitting room. I motioned that I'd get the door. I caught up with Dillon as he reached the library door.

"He probably wants to double-check your statement from last night. You'd had a lot to drink."

He just gave me a blank look as he knocked on the library door. I opened up the front door at almost the same time to find a nice-looking gentleman standing there, the raindrops bouncing like a rubber ball off his umbrella. He was wearing a pair of jeans and a blue and white striped shirt covered by a navy-blue jacket. He was around six feet tall with broad shoulders and a kind face. His brown hair was short, with just a little gray at the temples. He had a smile on his face and a twinkle in his eye that said he could be mischievous. I liked him immediately.

"May I help you?" I asked.

"Detective Gary Wright to see Detective Fitzgerald."

"Come in, please." I opened the door wider so he could walk in. "He's in with a witness. Do you want to interrupt him, or would you like a cup of tea first?"

"A cup of tea sounds wonderful. Thank you." He furled his umbrella and looked around for someplace to put it. I directed him to the umbrella stand in the corner where he placed it. I then noticed he was carrying a large, brown leather tote by the handles that looked cumbersome.

"You can set that there if you'd like," I pointed to the library door. He set the bag down, and he followed me to the breakfast room.

"Are you Molly?" We'd just walked into the breakfast room to find it empty, other than the maid who was cleaning up.

I looked at him and then at the maid. "Anna, is there any tea left?"

"Yes, miss. Half a pot. I thought I'd leave it for a little while in case anyone wanted some."

"Thank you."

I gave him a sly look. "Yes, I'm Molly." I poured a cup of tea and handed it to him. "There is both sugar and milk. Help yourself, detective."

"I must admit I have a bit of a sweet tooth," he said as he helped himself to some sugar.

"A man after my own heart," I replied as we sat down at the table. "Are you Detective Fitzgerald's partner?"

He took a sip of his tea, "Sometimes. It depends on the case."

"Yes, this one is a doozy, isn't it?" I smiled.

"A doozy?" He smiled. "I like it."

"Sorry, five years in the States, you pick up the slang."

"Did you know the victim?" he asked.

I laughed. "It's a long story, detective, but since you need to know, I'll tell you."

He pulled out his notebook and pen as I started my tale. When I was finished, I smiled at him. "As you can see, she had more enemies than friends."

"I can see how you think this is a—what did you say?—a 'doozy.'" He smiled.

"Yes, and I'm sure my brother will be your prime suspect." My smile turned into a frown.

He picked up his teacup and took a sip. "I won't lie to you. He is a person of interest, but we'll make sure we investigate everyone who had a motive."

"I have to say I'm relieved to hear you say that. One hears of police just clinging to the first viable suspect and not following leads." I took a sip of my tea.

Liam interrupted us as he arrived in the room. I couldn't help but feel a bit of a zing hit my heart when he smiled.

"Gary, good to see you." He looked at me. "Is there any tea left?" He went to the teapot and helped himself before coming and sitting down on the other side of the table. "Have you been here long?"

"Oh, my goodness! I forgot to ask Mrs. Jones to bring you that pitcher of water!" I looked at Gary, "Sorry to interrupt."

He winked at me as Liam said, "No problem. I sent the constable to ask her. We're all set, but I thought some tea would taste good about now."

Gary answered him, "Not long at all. Molly here was keeping me company." He winked at me again. "She filled me in on the victim. It appears we have quite a few possibilities."

Liam nodded, "And I've only spoken to three so far, Molly and her two siblings."

Gary looked at his notes. "Fiona was one of you who found the body, correct?" He looked at me, and I nodded. "And Dillon was dating the victim?"

"More like was trying to break up with her."

"What about the third person who found her?" Gary had put on his glasses and was skimming through his notebook.

Liam spoke up. "That would be Sergeant Murphy, the local police sergeant, and Molly's boyfriend."

I sighed, looking at Gary. "As in he's a boy and a friend, but he's not a boyfriend." I scowled at Liam, who was smiling.

"I've taken him off the case, but he's still on duty," Liam took a sip of this tea.

Gary stood up to refill his. "So, where do we stand now?"

Liam sighed. "Most of the guests are local. We still need to interview the guests staying here, and Mr. and Mrs.

Quinn. I had two constables take statements of the catering staff last night, and I just received those via email. As soon as we get the printer hooked up, I can print those out, and we can see who we may have to re-interview." He looked at me. "Is there someplace that Gary can do interviews?"

"Sure. He can use the parlor across from the library."

Gary was still standing by the teapot. "How many other witnesses do we need to interview?"

Liam said, "Well, there were 210 guests invited, so quite a few."

"I might be able to narrow that down some." They both looked at me. "Mum mentioned each person was given a ticket. I thought I would help you out and compare the ticket stubs to the list."

Gary and Liam looked at each other and then at me, making me nervous. "That is if you don't mind."

Liam took a sip of his tea, leaving Gary to answer. "We wouldn't mind at all. Thank you."

"The tickets are in the library. Once I get it figured out, I'll let you know."

"Thank you," Liam said. "Do you know where everyone is? I'd like to interview…" He looked at his notebook, "Jack and Jayne Webster." He looked from the notebook to Gary. "That name sounds familiar."

Gary looked at him and said, "If it's the Jayne Webster I'm thinking about, she's a judge in Cork."

"That's her. And her husband is a solicitor, same as my dad," I added.

Liam smiled at Gary. "In that case, you can interview her, and I'll take the husband."

"Don't forget about Aunt Agnes. Otherwise, she'll blow a gasket," I reminded him.

"I did tell her I'd talk to her before church, didn't I?" He thought for a moment. "If you see her, would you please tell her I'll see her right after Mr. Webster?"

I nodded as I got up from the table. "How about I find out where everyone is, and I'll send the Websters to you both. I'll also check with Mum on where the other three guests stayed last night."

"Thank you," they both said. I headed for the door, figuring they would prefer to be alone to talk about the really gritty stuff. I did, however, stop on the other side of the door for a moment to listen.

I heard a phone buzz, and a few seconds later, I heard Liam say, "No prints on the knife, but there was a concentration of dirt. They're running an analysis on it."

"It figures," Gary replied. "That would be too easy."

I heard some shuffling, and then Gary's voice. "So that's the Molly you met on the plane, is it?" He chuckled.

"Yes, that's her."

"At least you can stop searching for her now." I could hear him chuckling again.

"Let's stick with the case, shall we?" I heard Liam reply.

I heard footsteps coming down the hall, so I scurried away before I was caught. Two very interesting things—no prints on the knife and Liam had been looking for me. The last one made my heart do a little dance, even if it was due to bad circumstances. I went to the library where Constable Mills was sitting with a plate of cookies I'm sure he'd received from Mrs. Jones. He jumped up when I arrived.

"Can I help you, Miss Molly?" He was brushing cookie crumbs off his uniform.

"No, thank you, constable. I am just here to pick up something." The box was exactly where Dad said it was. I took it off the shelf and smiled. "Enjoy the cookies, constable."

I set the box on the table in the foyer before going to find out where everyone was.

After a quick search of the main floor, I found Dad, Jack, and Mr. Cooper in the sitting room discussing golf. I let Jack know the detective would like to speak to him and Jayne. Jack advised me Jayne was in her room and offered to let her know.

After perusing the second floor, everyone else appeared to be in their rooms. I stopped outside Aunt Agnes' room, and as I went to knock on the door, I heard raised voices. I stopped, and instead, placed my ear to the door. It didn't work, though. The voices were too muffled, so I knocked.

"Come in."

"Is everything okay?" Aunt Agnes had a vein pulsing in her forehead. Doreen's face was beat red, and she was wringing her hands.

"Everything is fine, dear. Is the detective ready to see me?" she asked.

"Almost. I thought I would stop by to tell you you're next." I looked from one to the other, almost afraid to leave them alone.

Doreen gave her grandmum a dirty look, said, "Excuse me," and raced out of the room.

Aunt Agnes held the door open for me, which I took as a polite way of asking me to leave, so I did, only to hear the door slam behind me.

I walked the short distance to the hallway to where my parents' room to find the door open. I walked in and found Mum sitting at her desk, her reading glasses perched on her nose, going through receipts.

"What is all the slamming doors about?"

"I'm not sure, but Aunt Agnes and Doreen were having a huge argument. How can Doreen stand it?"

Mum didn't take her eyes away from her task. She just said, "Ours is not to wonder why...."

"Well, how are you holding up? I put my arms around her neck and hugged her.

"Considering our charity gala ended with a murder, I'm carrying on." She turned around to look at me, slipping off her glasses.

I looked at the pile of receipts. "Did you make enough to get the church roof fixed?"

"Definitely. With a little to spare. It will go into the coffers. I'm sure it won't be long before something else breaks down. I'm sorry to say that church is falling apart."

"May I use your laptop again?" I asked. "I need to print a guestlist with everyone's ticket numbers."

"Already done, dear." She handed me some pages stapled together. "Here are two copies."

"Wonderful, thank you." I was glad she printed two. I could keep one in case I needed it.

Mum slipped her glasses on. "By the way, do you happen to know where the other three couples who came to the gala that weren't local stayed last night?"

She sighed, taking off her glasses again and rubbing the bridge of her nose. "I can't remember their names, but I know one stayed with the Andersons, one with the Kellys next door, and I believe the third couple stayed at the pub."

I kissed her on the cheek. "Thank you." I looked at my watch. "What time are we leaving for church?"

She looked out the window and said, "It depends on the weather. If it clears up, we can walk, so probably about ten-thirty. If it keeps raining, we'll be taking the cars, so probably about ten-forty." Her eyes went back to the receipts. "I'm trying to get an approximate total for Dad Kearney. He wants to announce it at mass."

I took the hint and left, heading back downstairs and grabbed the ticket box from the table on the foyer, and headed to the dining room. The first thing I did was write down the names and locations of the three couples and then began working on the list. Thirty minutes later, I stretched, beginning to feel the exhaustion of too little sleep set in. I needed tea, but first, I'd take the list to Liam. The library door was closed, but the sitting room was open, so I headed in there. Gary was sitting in the chair facing the door, his back to the fireplace, perusing his notes. I knocked on the door frame.

Gary looked up and motioned me in.

"Here is the updated guestlist. I've marked those who we don't have tickets for. It reduces your list by about thirty. I also marked those who are staying here, and marked where each of those people was as of about thirty minutes ago." I handed him the list. What I didn't say was I'd left the second copy that I was planning to keep in the dining room.

"Wonderful, Molly. Thank you. This will help. We'll get some constables on this list right away." He set the list on the table.

"Oh, I also have the information on where the three couples who aren't local stayed." I handed him the handwritten note.

His phone rang just then, and he said, "Excuse me."

I turned around to leave, but not before I heard him say, "Did you find anything?"

I once again lingered outside the door. "The will? Great, bring it by the station. Liam and I will be there around eleven."

Margery's will? They must have searched her house. I wonder who her beneficiary was. As far as I was aware, she didn't have any living relatives. I'd have to remember to ask. For now, I needed to check on Fiona.

I knocked on her door, and she opened it wide, motioning me inside. She still looked a little pale, and she was frowning. Rather than sitting, she paced up and down the room.

"How are you doing?" I asked as I walked in.

"I think I know who killed Margery." She kept pacing, now wringing her hands.

"What are you talking about?" I sat down on the bed.

She took a deep breath and repeated, "I think I know who killed her, Mol."

"Did you tell the detective?"

She shook her head and continued to pace. I took her by the arm and led her back to the bed where we both sat down.

"Start from the beginning."

She scooted farther back on the bed and turned toward me. "Remember how I told you that Aunt Agatha and Doreen sat at my table?"

I nodded.

"Margery was late. Did you notice?"

"Yes. She was all over Dillon. I felt sorry for him."

"Well, when she did, both Aunt Agnes and Doreen started acting strange."

"Acting strange how?"

"I don't know—they kept looking at each other and whispering. Then, Doreen didn't eat much of her dinner, and you know how strange that is."

"True, Doreen enjoys her meals."

"And like I said, she left right after dinner. Where did she go?"

"So, you think Doreen killed Margery? She did act strange at breakfast when they were told that Margery died."

"I don't know. I hope not, but if you'd seen the look on her face, Molly, it was pure hatred."

"Well, I can see how you would think that, but really? Doreen is such a—mousy type of person. I would think it Aunt Agnes before Doreen, don't you think?"

"I would except, remember, Aunt Agnes sat there talking my ear off until she saw some woman she was on a charity with and finally left the table. That was right before I found you."

"That may clear Aunt Agnes, but not necessarily Doreen. How do we know she was in her room? How much do we really know about Margery? I wish there was a way to find out more about her."

Chapter 14

Fiona said, "Do you have your laptop?"

"It's in my room."

Fiona hopped off the bed. "Come on."

I followed her through the bathroom and into my room, where I grabbed my laptop and signed in before handing it to her.

"Can you take notes?" she asked as she began to type.

"Sure." I grabbed my backpack, where I had a notebook and pen. I sat down on the seat of the vanity, ready to write.

"Here we go." She went quiet, but I could see her eyes moving across the screen. "Okay, we know she was here in town when she and Callum married, which was the same year as you and Keith. So, what? Five years ago?" She looked at me.

I nodded and wrote it down.

"Six months later, in November of that same year, they filed for divorce."

"Isn't that when she moved to Cork?" I asked.

"Yes—here it is." She continued reading.

I added that to my notes as she continued. "Two years later, on May 18, she married George Denton. Here is what the newspaper said, 'Mr. George Denton, 69, CEO of Denton Industries, married Margery Murphy, age 28, on May 18. Matron of honor was Lila Roberts, friend of the bride, best man was Joshua Denton, son of the groom. This is a second marriage for both.' It mentions George's daughter, Elizabeth Denton, didn't attend the wedding as she was living in Australia." She kept reading as I wrote it all down. "Then, it says what she was wearing, blah, blah, blah." She started typing again.

"Here we go. Six months later, on November 10, the body of George Denton was found dead in his home. The police called it a suspicious death, but although they questioned Mrs. Denton as a person of interest, she was never charged."

I wrote it all down and asked, "Anything else?"

"Give me a minute," she answered.

"Just how are you finding all of this out?"

She looked up from the screen and grinned, "You don't want to know." Her head went back to the screen, and a minute later, she said, "It looks like Margery's mum passed away shortly after that and left her the house here in Dooley, which explains why she moved back."

Just then, there was a knock on the door, but before I could say anything, it opened, and Mum said, "There you two are. Let's go. We're late." She left the door open and turned away.

I looked out the window and saw it had stopped raining and the sun was trying to shine through the clouds.

I put the notebook and pen in the desk drawer of my nightstand, Fiona closed the laptop, and we went downstairs.

Quite a crowd had gathered in the foyer. Mum and Dad were speaking with the two detectives. The Coopers and Websters were speaking to each other, and Aunt Agatha was at the front door speaking to the constable.

Liam turned to look at me as I reached the bottom of the stairs, and he smiled. I couldn't help but smile back as I reached his side. "Are all of your interviews finished?" I asked.

"Not yet. We're moving the investigation to the station in town. I've set up appointments with everyone who we haven't spoken to yet for this afternoon."

"We'd better get going, or Dad Kearney will be very displeased." Aunt Agnes shouted, slamming her cane on the floor a few times.

"Oh, dear, look at the time. We will be late," Mum said as she started toward the door.

Cars circled the drive, so I said, "I'm walking. Anyone else like to join me?"

Everyone except Aunt Agnes, Jack and Dad walked the short distance to the church.

I said to no one in particular, "Where's Doreen?"

Mum said, "She wasn't feeling well, so stayed behind."

Fiona and I looked at each other as we made our way down the driveway and a few blocks into town where the old stone church had stood for hundreds of years, its spire looming over the village.

The church bells were ringing as we walked up, and Dad Kearney was welcoming everyone into the church. He was smiling, but I could see his eyes were a little bloodshot. I'm sure if I looked closely, everyone here who attended the ball would have bloodshot eyes this morning, including me. Aiden and Ciara showed up with the children, and Kaleigh ran up to us. "Aunt Molly, Aunt Fiona! Can I sit with you?"

Ciara was right behind her and said, "Kaleigh, it's 'May I sit with you?'"

Kaleigh looked at her mum and said, "Mummy, I want to sit with the aunts. You can sit with daddy and the twins."

Ciara looked at us, frustration showing in her eyes as she said, "That's not what I meant. Sweetheart, you said 'can' I sit with you. You should have said, 'may' I sit with you."

Kaleigh took a deep breath and stared at her mother as she said, "May I sit with Aunt Fiona and Aunt Molly?"

I swung her up in my arms and said, "How about we all sit together?"

She wrapped her arms around me and said, "Okay, but not near my brothers. They're mean."

We walked into the church, and the scent of incense tickled my nose, and I was able to hold my sneeze until I put Kaleigh down. Then, I quickly grabbed a tissue from my purse, just in time.

Kayleigh looked at me and, in a rather loud voice, said, "Wow, that was a huge one, Aunt Molly. Bless you!"

I could feel everyone's eyes on me as we walked into the vestibule, dipped our fingers into the font of holy water, and made our way to our seats, genuflecting at the sign of the cross hanging over the altar.

Mass only lasted forty-five minutes, which I'm sure was only because our priest was hungover from the night before. During his "housekeeping" announcements, he thanked everyone who attended both the festival and the gala, telling the delightful news there were now enough funds to fix the church roof. At that, everyone cheered. We sang the final hymn and piled out of the church.

One of my favorite parts of mass is when everyone stands around outside, weather permitting, to catch up on the news from the week before. True, most of the villagers had mobile phones and could text, but there isn't anything as good as a face-to-face gab. The weather was still cooperating; the sun made it through the clouds, although I could see some darker ones off to the west. We'd probably have more rain later. But for now, I dug out my sunglasses from my purse and slipped them on my nose, just as I spotted Mrs. Riley talking to a young woman. I made my way over to her as the young lady walked away and gave her a hug.

"Good morning, Mrs. Riley," I said. I let her go. Her hand flew to her mouth, and her eyes were watery. "What's wrong?"

She looked around at the group and then whispered to me, "Is it true? That awful woman is dead?"

"Margery?" She nodded. "Yes, she is." I put my hand on her arm. "You're shaking. What's wrong? What can I do to help?"

She looked up at me, her eyes wide, and she whispered, "I know who did it."

"That seems to be popular." I smiled.

She looked up at me, "What?"

"Nothing. Did you tell the police?"

She shook her head. "Can you come have tea with me at the cottage? The bookstore is closed today, but I have to talk to someone about this."

"But are you sure you don't want me to take you to the police station now?"

"No, not yet. We can go after we talk this afternoon."

"Okay, I'll see you then. Do you need a ride home?"

The same woman who I'd seen at the bookstore covering for Mrs. Riley came up. "Beatrice, are you ready to go?"

"Molly, this is my friend Celia. She's driving me home."

The woman had short, curly red hair, and at her age, I doubt it was natural. "You're the one Beatrice is always talking about. It's nice to meet you." She held out her tanned hand, nails painted bright red.

"It's nice to meet you too, Mrs. ?"

"Baker, but you can call me Celia, everyone does."

"Well, Celia, thank you for seeing her home. She seems a bit shaken up."

"Bea, whatever is wrong?" she asked, concern on her face.

Mrs. Riley put a smile on her face and said, "Nothing a good cuppa won't fix, Celia. Let's get going," she said as she looked at me and said, "I'll see you at four, dear."

I was shaking my head when I walked back to the family, still gathered around together in front of the church, with one addition.

"Bethany! Good to see you." I bent over and gave her a hug. "I see you survived last night."

"I did. How about you two?" She looked from me to Fiona. "I heard you found Margery's body. That had to be awful!"

"It wasn't pleasant, that's for sure," Fiona added. "How is Mrs. Riley? I saw you speaking to her."

"I'm not sure. She's really upset. She says she knows who killed Margery." I heard several gasps and looked around. I hadn't realized I'd said it so loud, but several pairs of eyes were on me.

"Did she say who?" asked Fiona.

I shook my head and then lowered my voice. "I'm sure it's not who you were thinking. She doesn't even know that person."

Bethany looked at me and then Fiona. "What are you two talking about?"

Fiona spoke up. "She's talking about me." She lowered her voice to a whisper, "I thought our cousin Doreen might have been the murderer, but Molly convinced me that I was imagining things."

"I guess I'll find out later. I'm meeting her for tea at four."

"Isn't she going to go to the police?" Jayne asked.

I shook my head. "She wants to wait until we talk."

Bethany added, "I really like Mrs. Riley. I spend a lot of time in her bookstore, so I hope she's okay." She then looked at her watch. "I have to go. I don't have to work today, but I have a ton of laundry to do, and I have to return my catering uniform by five."

She and Fiona hugged as Fiona said, "I have to pack up my things and get home and tackle laundry too. What happened to Sunday being a day of rest?" There were a few chuckles as we all said our goodbyes, and we started walking toward home.

"I don't understand why we need to stay here. Neither Rob nor I had anything to do with the murder. We didn't even know the girl," Bryn whined. "I have a hair appointment tomorrow that I just cannot miss!"

Mum said, "I'm sure you can reschedule your appointment, Bryn."

"I don't know. She's awfully hard to get an appointment with." She pulled out her phone.

I looked at Jayne, who was rolling her eyes, and I smiled.

As we walked, I slid my arm through Jayne's and said, "Where's Jack?"

"Oh, rode back in the car with your dad. Saving his energy for golfing, I guess." She sighed.

"A penny for your thoughts," I didn't want to interfere, but she hadn't been herself since she spotted Margery last night.

She looked at me and smiled. "They're not even worth a halfpenny, my dear."

"Oh, I don't know. I think sharing your thoughts with an unbiased person is worth a great deal," I answered.

She put her hand over mine and said, "You really are a dear. That sounds like something your mum would say. She's so proud of you."

"I doubt she's very proud of me at the moment. Failed marriage, no idea where my life is leading me. I'm more like one of her lost sheep."

"It takes a lot more courage to walk away from a poor relationship than it does to stay in one," Jayne said as we stopped before crossing the street.

"May I ask you a question?" I said as we continued to walk.

She nodded and said, "I may not answer it."

"How did you know Margery?"

She took in a deep breath and said, "We knew her husband George and his first wife. It was so tragic when she died. It was a drunk driver, never found. It devastated him. We ran in the same circles, attended the same parties. We were all shocked when he married someone so much younger than himself, but we all agreed to give her a chance and make her feel welcome. She, however, was a venomous bitch. It didn't take her long to discover everyone's secrets. I have it on good authority she was a blackmailer."

"You're kidding? Did she try to blackmail you?" I asked.

She laughed. "As a judge, I can't have any secrets, so she had nothing on me, but she did on a wonderful friend of mine. I wanted to help, but she wouldn't let me. She ended up committing suicide, so I have nothing good to say about Margery Denton."

"Too bad you couldn't arrest her for blackmail. I can understand why you hate her. I was thinking she was Jack's mistress." I chuckled, keeping my eyes on the pavement as we walked.

She sighed. "She was, but I didn't know that until last night. When George died, and she was accused, she turned to Jack for help. It turned out the police didn't have enough evidence, and they let her go. Shortly after, she moved away." She looked at me and stopped again in the driveway. "Last night, she pulled me aside and gleefully filled me in on her time with Jack."

"That witch! Jayne, I'm so sorry."

"That's okay. I did kind of burst her bubble when I told her I knew all about the affair and how Jack had ended it shortly after it started. I just didn't tell her I didn't know it was her."

"Does Jack know she told you?"

She nodded. "I told him last night. He was furious! If the two of us hadn't been together all night, I would think he did it, but he doesn't have a cruel bone in his body."

"Did you tell the police?"

"Yes. I am waiting for them to show up and haul me away in handcuffs." A look of worry flashed over her face.

"If they do, I promise to have Mrs. Jones bake a cake with a file in it," I said, smiling. "But seriously, I won't lie and say that isn't an excellent motive, but there are other people with good motives too."

She nodded. "I just hope the police will do their jobs and find the killer."

We'd reached the house at that point, all filing in and going our separate ways.

Shortly afterward, Fiona and Dillon left for their own homes. I waved as they left, telling Fi I'd talk to her soon. Mrs. Jones served a quick lunch of soup and sandwiches, and then I grabbed my laptop and hopped up on my bed, stacking pillows behind me. I opened up the document from earlier and revised my list.

Callum Murphy married to Margery, divorced after six months. Doesn't appear to have any feelings for her at all, let alone murderous ones.

Beatrice Riley wouldn't sell the bookstore to her, didn't like her because she was a "hussy" and was an unpleasant customer. Thinks she knows who the killer is.

Dillon Quinn broke up with Margery, but she wouldn't accept it. Had an argument with victim before she was killed. (What time was she killed?)

Scott, the bartender, wasn't fond of her, but why? Because she wouldn't leave Dillon alone, or did he date her as well at some point?

Jayne Webster knew George Denton, and the victim had an affair with Jack.

Jack Webster furious at Margery because she told Jayne about the affair.

Doreen Quinn just where did she go when she left dinner?

I felt confident that none of these people would have done it, but who else was there? I wracked my brain trying to come up with someone else, heck, anyone else, I could add to the list. What do I do now? I thought back once again to my mystery training via books and television. I needed to search Margery's house. I closed the laptop and pulled out my lock picking set from where I'd stashed it in the vanity. I stuck it in the back pocket of my jeans and covered it with my blouse. I made my way downstairs and asked Mum once again if I could use her car.

Chapter 15

I stopped at the local drugstore, purchased some plastic gloves, and continued toward the house that previously belonged to Margery's parents. I remember being invited to a birthday party there. I didn't want to go, but Mum made me. I had a pleasant time, but only because Ciara and Reanna were there too. I parked a few blocks away and walked toward Center Street, trying to blend in, looking like I was just taking a stroll. I stopped when I came upon a sky-blue house with white trim. The front yard needed mowing, but there were flowers around the front porch and not a weed in sight.

I walked down the driveway to the back door, stopping to put on my gloves. A few minutes later, I was in a kitchen painted mint green with oak cabinets. The counters were bare of clutter other than a coffee pot. I walked through to the living room, and it too was uncluttered, no magazines or papers lying around. I followed the hallway until I came to two doors. One was a bathroom, the other looked like an office. The desk was empty of clutter, just a printer and a few computer cords. The police must have taken her computer. I went through the drawers but found nothing of interest. No files titled "people who want to kill me," just credit card receipts and other bill receipts that looked like Margery had printed off her computer. There was one file that had her divorce decree from Callum, and the death certificate for George, the cause of death, said, "insulin overdose." No wonder they thought it was murder.

I went through the closet, but it was full of winter clothes. I left that room and went upstairs, where there were three more bedrooms. The largest one looked to be Margery's. I was glad there was more clutter here, clothes strewn around, a book on the nightstand. I went through the closet and found a shoebox on the shelf. I brought it down and opened it up. It was full of photos. I sat down on the bed and went through them. They went back quite a few years. There were pictures of when she was young, family pictures of her and her parents, even pictures from the birthday party I'd attended. There were pictures of her and Callum on a vacation somewhere. They were both smiling, dressed in swimsuits and straw hats. At least they appeared to have had some good times. Then, I found pictures of her with George. I assumed it was George. He was older, with gray hair and a bit of a paunch, but in all the photos, he was smiling. There was a photo of Margery, George, and an adolescent. I looked on the back, and it had "Margery, George and Josh Denton" written on it. That must be the stepson. He was taller than his dad, with light hair and slim. There was another closeup picture of what must have been a Halloween party. I flipped it over, and it said, "Josh and Elizabeth, ages 12 and 10." Josh was dressed as a cowboy, and Elizabeth a fairy. The paint on her face was blue and pink to match her costume, her white wings gleaming with glitter, her blonde hair up in a bun. The next picture I came to was a close up of a tattoo. On the back, it said, "Elizabeth's tattoo. What was she thinking?" It was a blue unicorn located on the top of her left shoulder. The writing was different from Margery's. Elizabeth's mum, perhaps? I wonder why Margery kept them?

As interesting as the photos were, they weren't answering any of my questions. If I were trying to hide something, where would I hide it? I looked through the vents, but couldn't see anything stashed behind them. Then, I remembered a conversation between Margery and Reanna when we were about sixteen. One of our other classmates, Sloane something, had gotten grounded because her mum had found marijuana in her bedroom. Margery told Sloane how stupid she was, and told her every teen knows they should have a secure hiding place no one would think of. However, I don't recall her ever saying where it was.

I pulled my phone out of my pocket and called Reanna. She picked up on the second ring.

"Hey, Molly. What's up?" Her voice sounded scratchy.

"Did I wake you up?"

"No. Just drank a little bit too much whiskey. Don't ever let me do that again," she moaned.

"I think I recall you saying that once before when we were about twenty. We'd gone to that party down at the beach…"

"Ya, ya okay, so I like whiskey. Hey, I heard there was some commotion at the party last night. Anything exciting happen? We left around midnight, but my nosy neighbor woke me up two hours ago, asking for details. She was very disappointed I didn't have any."

"That's why I'm calling, actually. Someone murdered Margery Denton last night."

"Really? We must have already left. I knew no one liked her, but who would have hated her that much?"

"That's an excellent point. Who did hate her enough to kill her? We didn't like her, but that's because she irritated us. None of us hated her enough to kill." I would have to think about that later. "That's not why I'm calling, though. Do you remember when we were teens, and Margery mentioned she had a hiding place that no one would find?"

"Vaguely, why?"

"I'm at Margery's house trying to get some clues to who killed her, but I can't find anything."

"You should leave this to the police. Wait. I forgot who I'm talking to. Check the floor."

I looked down at the dark-blue carpet. "The floor?"

"She used to have a loose floorboard. She would hide stuff in there she didn't want her parents to find."

"Really? How did you know that?" I left the bedroom, looking for a room with bare floors.

"I heard it from someone. I can't remember who. I only remember it because I tried doing it myself, but we didn't have any bare floors."

"Thank you! I appreciate your help. I should probably see if I can find it and get the heck out of here."

"Okay, but be careful!"

"I will." I disconnected the call as I found a bedroom that had hardwood floors. I laid down on my stomach, trying to see if there were any disturbances in the floor, and I could see a corner slightly higher than the rest located right near the double bed. I looked around for something to pry it with, deciding to try my lock pick. It took me a few tries, but it worked.

The area below was about ten inches by seven inches across. There were two notebooks, along with some thumb drives. I set the notebooks aside and looked closer at the memory sticks. Each one had a piece of tape covering it, each with a set of initials and a date. What on earth was she up to? No drugs, although there wasn't a reason for her to hide those, so why hide this stuff? I sat on the bed and opened a notebook. It was her journal. I went to the last couple of pages and read.

She's moved back to Dooley. Damn her! I guess the little princess's marriage broke up, and she's come back to

Mommy and Daddy. I just know she's convinced Dillon to break up with me. She hates me enough to do it!

The next day's entry, the last entry dated the day before she died, said, "*Can you believe that bitch from boutique sold my dress! And after all the business I've given her. I'll never shop there again. Now, I have nothing to wear to the gala, and I have to look my best, I just know Dillon will propose!*"

I closed the book with the realization Margery had been demented. How could she think Dillon would propose? I opened the second book. Each page had line after line filled with initials and money payments ranging from €500 to €5000. Wow—Jayne was right. Margery was blackmailing people. I compared the initials on the thumb drives to the initials in the book, and they matched. I searched for the thumb drive correlating with the €5000 payment in the book and stuck it in my pocket. I put the rest of them back into the floor but kept out both notebooks. I'm sure Liam would love to see these. They should offer a few more suspects.

I had just put the plank into place when I thought I heard a noise downstairs. I stopped to listen again. Sure enough, someone was walking around downstairs. Crap! I knew enough not to panic, but that didn't stop my heart from practically jumping out of my chest. I took a deep breath and let it out slowly. Run or hide? Two suitable options. I got up and looked out the window. There was a roof I could jump out on, but it faced the front of the house, and the entire neighborhood would see me. Okay, hiding it is. I could hear the footsteps coming up the stairs, so I quickly scooted under the bed. Chances are whoever it was would check Margery's room first, but running wasn't an option unless they closed the door. Otherwise, they would see me run by. Best to stay here for now. As clean as Margery kept the house—or most likely a housekeeper, they didn't clean under the beds very well. The wooden floor was dusty, and I could feel a sneeze coming on. I moved my finger to my nose, almost in time, but not quite. A slight noise escaped, and I held my breath.

I saw feet walk in the room—brown work boots and light-colored jeans. The feet stopped, and my heart gave a jolt. It would take a lot of explaining if anyone found me here. I don't think anyone would believe I was the dust bunny police. The feet turned around and left. I let out the breath I didn't realize I'd been holding, and I set my forehead on the cool, dusty floor in relief. I lifted my head back up when I heard steps on the stairs again. I quickly scooted out from under the bed and ran to a room with a view on the backside of the house, pulling out my phone, ready to take photos. A few minutes later, a well-built man with blond hair, dressed in a light-blue long-sleeve polo shirt, jeans, and work boots, strolled away down the walkway and scooted through the hedge to the house behind. I quickly took some pictures, but since he didn't turn around, I wasn't sure if anyone could identify him. I slipped my phone back in my pocket, gathered up my evidence, and left through the back door, making sure I locked it. Thankfully, the rain had stopped, so hopefully, I looked like I was taking a casual stroll as I made my way to where I'd parked the car instead of someone who just committed breaking and entering.

The digital clock in Mum's car was glaring at me, reminding me I only had ten minutes to get to Mrs. Riley's, or I'd be late. I'd parked on the side of a narrow road, two tires on the curb, so I did a quick look in the mirror and did a U-turn, heading toward the sea. Mr. and Mrs. Riley had purchased a small cottage on a cliff overlooking the sea quite a few years ago. I remember the two of them being so excited about fulfilling their dream of someday owning a home on the water. Mrs. Riley would talk about the pleasant time she and Mr. Riley would sit in their garden and watch all the boats come and go into Dooley Harbor. I hadn't been to the cottage in ages and couldn't wait to see it again.

I pulled into the gravel driveway of Rose Cottage with one minute to spare, except Mrs. Riley drilled into me how if you're not five minutes early, you're late. The whitewashed cottage sparkled in the afternoon sun. The first thing I'd noticed was they'd built a garage, the door painted candy-apple red. They'd also painted the shutters and front door to match. At the same time, they must have extended the porch to where it now went from the edge of the house all the way to the beginning of the garage. There were flower boxes attached to the porch railing, wave petunias hanging out, their bright colors a nice welcome to those coming to visit.

Roses, which the cottage was named after, were planted along the walkway from the driveway to the porch. The red, yellow, and blue roses were in different stages of growth. The red ones were dying, the yellow ones in full bloom, and the blue ones beginning to bud.

I took a deep breath, letting the sweet fragrance fill my lungs. Along with the salt air, I felt some tension from the past few days melt away.

I walked up the steps and onto the porch. On one side of the door, there was a white wicker swing with a red cushion along with two matching chairs. On the other end was a matching patio table with two chairs. They were all placed allowing a delightful view of the small woodland in front of the house. I walked up the stairs and used the brass knocker to announce my arrival. Waiting a minute or two, when nothing happened, I knocked again. When she still didn't answer, I went around to the back, thinking she was pulling weeds and forgot the time. That would be just like her.

The yard was surrounded by a large stone fence you see all over Ireland, but there was a gap between the stone fence and the house, so she'd added a white, wooden fence with a very sturdy gate. I walked through it and felt like I'd walked into a greenhouse, flowers, trees, and shrubs everywhere. This was definitely all new. She'd had a small patch of flowers when I was here last. I had stepped onto a concrete path when I'd walked through the gate. I could go straight, toward the sea, or right took me behind the house to a large patio, where there sat an enormous table and chairs, large enough for eight people at least, an unfurled umbrella sticking out of the middle. Looking back at the house, there was a set of sliding glass doors leading into the kitchen. Looking out at the sea, there was another path that took me down the middle of the yard, where I could see a huge, raised gazebo standing. Normally it was very windy back here, but they'd planted sturdy tress, now about twenty feet high, along both sides around the corners to cut the wind and protect the garden. Smart thinking on their part. I followed the path to the gazebo and walked up the steps. I could see a head peeking out over a chair. I'd finally found Mrs. Riley.

"Mrs. Riley, this is gorgeous! I can't believe how much it's changed since I was here last." I looked out over the water where I could see a few boats out, some just tiny specks on the horizon. I could identify sailboats and speedboats, their motors barely heard over the seagulls and other flying creatures, making the most of this beautiful day. I walked over to the bench and laid my hand on her shoulder. "Did you fall asleep?" I asked aloud, expecting her to laugh at me and admonish me for being late. Instead, she fell over, blood-soaked into her blouse, her eyes wide open in shock, her throat slit.

Chapter 16

I felt my stomach churn, the nausea rising until I could feel it burn in the back of my throat. I swallowed. This can't be happening, not Mrs. Riley. Who would do this? Why would someone do this? I turned away, stumbling, following the path that just a few moments ago brought me joy, stumbling through the gate. My hands shook as I took the phone from my pocket and found Callum's name.

"Hiya, Molly. Do you miss me?" the deep voice asked.

I closed my eyes to try to erase the image now burned into my memory. "It's Mrs. Riley, Callum. She's—dead. Murdered. Oh my God, who would have done such a thing?" The tears ran down my face as I tried to take deep breaths.

"Molly, where are you?" His voice had quickly gone from flirty to police mode.

"I'm at Mrs. Riley's house. We'd planned on having tea, but she's—"

"Molly, stay put. I'll be right there. And don't touch anything."

I'm not sure how long I stood there looking at my phone when I finally stuck it in my back pocket. Looking around, how could everything have changed so much, yet everything looks the same? I was leaning against Mum's car, letting the tears roll down my face when I heard the wail of a siren. A few seconds later, a white Garda car pulled in, a black Miata right behind it.

Callum jumped out of his car as soon as it stopped and came over to me, taking me in his arms. I laid my head on his shoulder, closed my eyes, and tried to get ahold of my emotions. When I opened them again, Liam was standing behind Callum, a look on his face I couldn't read.

"Sergeant Murphy, please secure the scene," said Liam.

Callum let me go, but my eyes were on Liam. I could feel Callum's eyes on me as he said, "Yes, sir."

He touched my arm and asked, "Where is she?"

I looked toward the back yard, pointed, and said, "In the gazebo." He walked away.

I turned my head back around to find Liam now standing in front of me. He laid his hand on my arm and said, "You need to sit down. You're awfully pale."

I laughed through the tears. "Well, finding two bodies in two days will do that to a person." I looked up into his face, and my heart did a little flip. There was a look on his face I hadn't seen before. Was it concern?

His hand moved down my arm to my hand, and he pulled me into his arms. The emotions I'd been trying to control crumbled, and I cried on his chest.

A few minutes later, I'd cried myself out and pushed away from him, but not totally out of his embrace, and I looked at his face. "Who would do such a thing?"

"I don't know, but we'll find out." His eyes searched mine. For what, I wasn't sure.

Our attention was diverted by someone clearing their throat. We looked toward the sound. "Sir, you need to see this. It's awful."

I looked over, and Callum's face was white as a Michigan snow. Liam led me to the porch. I sat down on the loveseat, and then he disappeared. I could feel a throbbing on the left side of my head like someone had placed an ice pick into my skull. I threw decorum to the wind, curling up on the swing. Placing my head on the small pillow, I closed my eyes. I heard more sirens and doors opening and closing, but I laid there trying to ignore it all until I felt someone sit down beside me.

"Molly, are you okay?" Fiona took my hand, and I opened my eyes. Bethany was there too, sitting on one of the chairs, her eyebrows bunched together, her lips tight. I sat up straight, placing my feet back on the ground.

"No, I'm not. Who could do such a thing?" Tears once again fell down my face.

"I don't know," answered Bethany, "but I hope they're brought to justice. First Margery, and now this? What is happening to this town?" I could see her jaw tighten as she tried to control her anger.

"Can we take you home?" Fiona asked.

"Um, I don't know. They haven't asked me questions yet, so I'm not sure."

Bethany jumped up and said, "I'll go find out."

We both watched her go, and then I laid my head back as I asked, "Who called you?"

"Callum. He thought someone should be here with you." She hadn't let go of my hand, for which I was grateful.

I looked at our clasped hands and said, "Thank you for being here. You're the anchor keeping me from going adrift."

"I wouldn't be anywhere else, sis. It helps that your sexy cop is here too." She smiled at me.

"Yes, that was quite the surprise," I answered. "Would you be a dear and grab some aspirin out of my purse?"

"Sure." She looked around. "Where is it?"

"It's in the car."

While Fiona did that, Liam walked up to the porch, Bethany, behind him. He sat down beside me and asked, "Feeling better?"

"Splitting headache. Fiona is getting me some aspirin."

"Do you feel up to talking about it?"

I closed my eyes tight to stop the tears from falling again. I nodded.

Fiona chose that moment to hand me the bottle of aspirin and a bottle of water she'd found somewhere. I opened the bottle, took two out, and swallowed them down with some water. I screwed the top back on it and set it beside me.

Fiona and Bethany were sitting in the chairs on each side of the swing. Liam pulled out his notebook.

"What time did you arrive?"

"A little before four."

"Had you made plans to meet?" he asked.

I went over the story and said, "I told her she needed to go to the police, but she said she wanted to talk to me about it first." I closed my eyes, sickened at how I'd reacted. "I laughed at the entire thing. Oh my God, this is my fault." I said, placing my thumb and forefinger on my head, trying to stop the shooting pain and closing my eyes.

"Molly, this isn't your fault!" Fiona exclaimed, "and you were only laughing because of me."

Liam looked from one to the other. "What are you talking about?"

Fiona explained, "I'd already given her my silly version of the killer, and then right after that, Mrs. Ryan does the same thing. No wonder she didn't take it seriously."

Liam took a deep breath and said, "I need you to go over it one more time, and then you can go home. Okay?"

I went over everything again, and he asked, "So you never went inside?"

"No," I answered. "I just knocked on the door. When she didn't answer, I went around back."

"And you didn't see anyone else around?"

"Not a soul. All I was thinking was how peaceful and gorgeous it was. I didn't notice anyone or any vehicles."

Liam flipped his notebook closed and said, "You can go, but I might have questions for you later." He looked at Fiona. "Can you take her home?"

"Sure." She looked at Bethany. "Can you drive Mum's car?"

"Sure," she said.

Fiona led me to her car, asking for Mum's keys. I handed them over and watched as she gave them to Bethany, who followed us back to the house.

Neither Fiona nor I spoke on the short ride back to the manor. Once we arrived, I didn't make it any farther than the parlor, where I kicked off my shoes, laid down on the couch, and closed my eyes. I felt a blanket covering me. Someone stuck a pillow under my head, and I fell asleep.

When I woke up, the room was lit up. Like most of the rooms on this side of the house, it had floor to ceiling windows overlooking the now dark garden. Grandma Kennedy was sitting across from me, knitting. The yarn was the same color as Liam's eyes. Thinking about Liam made me think about Mrs. Riley, and I closed my eyes tight again, trying to erase the image of her surprised face and slit throat.

"Aye, you're awake." Her knitting needles clicked with each stitch.

I sat up, throwing off the blanket and stretching the kinks out of my neck. "What are you doing here?"

"I can't come visit my daughter and granddaughter for no apparent reason?" she said, her wrinkled face smiling.

The smile I gave her was brief. "It's good to see you, Gran."

She stopped knitting for a moment to ring the bell I hadn't noticed was on the table. A few minutes later, Mum, Fiona, Bethany, Jayne, and Aunt Agnes all converged on the parlor.

Mum sat down beside me and pulled me into her arms. "Oh, my darling. How are you doing?"

"I'm not sure." I laid my head on her shoulder for a moment before asking the crowd, "Any word from the police?"

Fiona said, "Callum called to check on you, but he didn't give any details, but then, I didn't ask."

Mrs. Jones came in with a tray of tea and sandwiches. "You must be starving, Miss Molly." She set it down, and Fiona poured me a cup, added the required sugar and handed it to me, as Mum took a plate, added a sandwich, and set that on the table in front of me.

"Thank you." I took a sip of tea and realized everyone was looking at me. "I'm fine, really. It was quite a shock, and it will take a while to get it over it, but really, you don't have to worry about me."

It took me eating a sandwich and drinking two cups of tea to get everyone to relax. One by one, most everyone left, leaving Fiona and Bethany. Once we were alone, Bethany picked up her purse that was sitting at her feet and pulled something out of it.

"I think these are yours. I found them on the passenger seat of your mum's car, and I didn't think you wanted her to see them."

She handed me the two notebooks and the thumb drive. I took them and said, "Thank you. You're right."

"What are those, Molly?" Fiona asked.

"I'm not sure yet. Just something I found at Margery's house. I'll look at them later." We all stood up. "Thank you so much for coming for me. I really appreciate it." I gave them both a hug and said, "But now I think I need to be alone to process it all if you don't mind."

"We understand, don't we, Bethany?"

"Yes. You've had to deal with a lot of stuff these past two days," Bethany answered.

"Tell you what. Why don't we get together tomorrow night? Fiona, if I can use your house, I'll make you two dinner. How does that sound?"

They looked at each other, and Fiona said, "That sounds great. Why don't you drop by my office tomorrow and pick up the key? I get out of work at half-past four." She looked at Bethany, "What time do you need to work tomorrow?"

"I don't have to be at the restaurant until six, so that sounds perfect."

We said our goodbyes. I took the notebooks and went upstairs.

I took a shower and got into my pajamas, settling on my bed with my laptop and the two notebooks and read Margery's journal. I looked out the window and noticed it was raining again. It fit my mood perfectly.

The date of the first entry was two months ago when she'd begun dating Dillon. She wrote how much of a gentleman he was, how kind he was to her. It made me wonder if that was unusual in her relationships.

I kept reading. Most of it was how wonderful Dillon was and how she was sure he was going to propose. There were a few entries concerning people in the village and how they all hated her. The butcher who gave her inferior meat, the dry cleaners she thought lost a piece of her clothing on purpose. Reanna, who had always been inferior to her in every way, could make a go of that "little sweet shop." I then read how she wanted to buy Mrs. Riley's bookstore so she could show the village how she, too, could run a profitable shop. She dedicated the last few pages to me and how much she hated me and blamed me for Dillon wanting to break up with her.

I grabbed the thumb drive and inserted it into my computer. It was a sex tape, just as I expected. I didn't know who he was, but I recognized him. He was the man who I'd seen in Margery's house the same time I was there. But who was he?

My head was throbbing again, so I put everything away, took two more aspirin, and went to bed.

# # #

I woke up on Monday morning to the sound of rain tapping against my bedroom window. I glanced at the ominous sky and realized it would most likely rain all day. I dressed in a pair of jeans and an old peach, oversized crewneck Aran sweater, hoping the bright color would help cheer me up.

I planned to hand the notebooks over to Liam, but I wanted to make copies first, so I went into Mum's sitting room and used her copier/scanner/printer and copied several pages of both the journal and the notebook. Once I finished, I stuck the pages in my backpack and stashed it back in the closet.

I texted Callum, asking him for Liam's number. He texted it to me a few minutes later, asking me how I was. I told him I was doing okay, still very upset about what happened. Then I asked if they'd received a time of death for Mrs. Riley. He took so long I didn't think he would respond. A few minutes later, I received a text that said, "between 1p-3p." I texted Liam next, asking if I could see him. He texted back right away he'd be here in thirty minutes.

I made my way downstairs, determined to put on a smiling face. Everyone was there, all in various stages of eating breakfast. I went to the sideboard, filled my plate, and sat down next to Doreen.

"How are you today, Doreen?"

She pushed up her glasses, giving me a brief smile, "Fine. How are you?"

I honestly wasn't sure. The past few days seemed so surreal. Did I really find two dead bodies? Were they connected? They had to be. I realized I hadn't answered Doreen. "Oh, I'm good. What are you going to do today?"

"I think I'll go to the library and read. You have a lovely collection of books."

I nodded. "If it was up to Dad, it would be full of farming and law books. However, we were a household of readers, so hopefully, you'll find something. I know there are quite a few mysteries, my favorite genre, that I left here when I went to America."

I stabbed my eggs with my fork and realized I really was hungry. I hadn't eaten since lunch yesterday, other than the sandwich I had last night.

I just finished my breakfast when Higgins came to me and whispered, "Detective Fitzgerald is here to see you."

I wiped my face with my napkin and said, "Please show him into the parlor, Higgins, and tell him I'll be right there. Would you offer him some tea?"

"Yes, miss."

I excused myself and went upstairs to grab the notebooks, but not the thumb drive. I wanted to show it to

Fiona and Bethany tonight at dinner to see if they recognized the man. I added some lipstick and made my way downstairs to the parlor. I walked in, and Liam was sitting on the same couch I'd slept on last night. He stood up when I entered.

The dark-blue suit looked good on him. I looked into his handsome face and said, "Good morning."

"Good morning to you. How are you doing this morning?" His eyes examining every detail of my face. It made me glad I put on some lipstick.

"I won't lie to you. I'm feeling quite— discombobulated, for lack of a better word. It's been a rough week. Thank you for coming to see me."

"I was planning on coming, anyway. I wanted to let your guests know they're free to leave."

"They'll be happy to hear that. Does this mean you've figured out who killed Margery? Who?"

He pinched his lips together. "You know I can't tell you."

I nodded my head. "Most everyone is in eating breakfast. Why don't we go give them the good news?"

A few minutes later, we were back in the parlor. He sat on the couch again, and I sat in a chair across from him. I had sat the notebooks down on the table before we left, and he looked at them, then at me.

"What are those?" he asked.

"Before I explain," I said, "You have to promise you won't arrest me."

Chapter 17

His eyes narrowed. "Will I have reason to arrest you?"

"Maybe." I picked up the notebooks, holding them in my hands.

"What did you do?" He leaned toward me, his elbows on his knees, his hands clasped in front of him.

"Well, I kind of broke into Margery's house."

"Kind of? The lock picking set from your grandmum?"

I smiled. "Yes. It's nice to know I haven't lost my touch."

He didn't smile back, just held out his hand for the books, so I handed them over.

"Where did you find these? I had the house searched." He flipped through the journal. He then set it down and flipped through the second book, his eyebrows raised.

"You wouldn't have found it. She had a secret compartment in the floor of a bedroom. I only knew about it because of something that happened when we were younger." I didn't mention Reanna. No reason bringing her into it. "I left the thumb drives there if you want to send someone to collect them." Each one had a piece of tape with initials written on them, and I noticed they match the initials in one notebook.

He placed the notebook back on the coffee table and pulled his phone off his belt. A few seconds later, he was barking orders to someone. He then looked at me and mouthed, "Where is it?"

"Have them check the bedroom without carpeting. There's a loose floorboard between the nightstand and the bed."

He repeated what I told him into the phone and then hung up. "Thank you, but please stay out of this and leave it to the police."

I almost rolled my eyes. I had expected to hear that at some point. "Of course, I will. Now, what do you want to know about yesterday?"

He pulled out his notebook. "Do you know if Mrs. Riley had any family?"

"I don't think so. She and Henry had no children or siblings, as far as I know. Unless there is a long-lost relative, I doubt it. Check with Celia Baker. She is—" I swallowed, "was a friend of Mrs. Riley. She's the one who drove her to church yesterday."

He wrote the name in his notebook. "Do you know if she had any enemies?"

I felt the tears start to form. I swallowed again and looked at the tea tray. Thankfully, Mrs. Jones had included an extra cup. I quickly poured myself a cup and took a sip. "As far as I know, everyone loved her." I set the cup down on the table and started to pace. "Who would do this?"

"We'll figure it out. Can you sit back down, please?"

I sat back down. "Sorry, nervous habit."

"Do you have any idea who her beneficiary is?"

"Beneficiary? No idea. I don't even know if she had a will—or a lawyer." I tried to think back to conversations we'd had over the years. I didn't recall the subject ever coming up.

He closed his notebook and tucked it back in his pocket. He picked up a briefcase from the side of the couch, opened it, took out a yellow legal pad and a pen, and slid them over to me. "I need you to write everything down that happened yesterday."

I picked them up and started writing. Twenty minutes later, my hand had a cramp, but I finished and pushed the notebook toward him. He picked it up and slid it in his briefcase. "I'll have this typed up for you to sign." He then pulled out a folder. He opened it up and took out some papers. "Here is your statement from Margery's murder. Can you read it over, and if it's correct, sign it, please?"

A few minutes later, I signed it and handed it to him. He slid it in his briefcase and said, "I have something to tell you now."

"Okay, what is it?"

"I shouldn't be telling you this, but we're bringing Dillon in as a person of interest in Margery's murder."

As my stomach sank, my blood boiled. I flew out of the chair and started pacing again. "He didn't do it!"

Liam stood up too and came over to me, taking me by the shoulders. "He's not under arrest—yet. But he's the most viable suspect, and I'm sure if you could think rationally, you'd realize that."

"Rationally?" I retorted. I closed my eyes, memories of Keith using that same word flooding my brain. I pulled myself out of his grip and started pacing again. "Why is it when a woman has an opinion different from a man's, she's being irrational?" I turned and looked at him.

His jaw tightened, "Look, I understand you've had a rough couple of days. Most people don't come across one dead body in their lifetime, let alone two. All I'm saying is if you look at it from a police point of view, he has motive, means, and opportunity."

"He didn't do it," I repeated, but much less vehemently.

He walked over to the table and picked up the notebooks I'd given him and slipped them in his briefcase as well. "If what I suspect about that notebook is correct, you've given us more people to check out. I just need you to trust me."

I wanted to, but this was my brother we're talking about. Even though I told him I'd stay out of it, I couldn't, not with my brother's life at stake.

He gathered up the folder and the notebooks and placed them in his briefcase.

"The statement will be available for you to sign soon. I'll call you." He walked toward the door.

"I'll see you out." I watched him run through the rain to his car. A few seconds later, he was driving away.

I turned around to see Doreen on the stairs holding onto the banister so tightly her fingers were white. "Is he gone?" she asked.

"You mean the detective?"

She nodded.

"Yes, he is. Why don't you come join me in the library? I'll point out some of my favorite books."

She smiled and came down to the bottom of the stairs. I opened the library door, and we went in. Her eyes perused the shelves, the first true smile on her face I'd seen since she arrived.

"You love books as much as I do, it seems. What type of books do you like to read?"

"It varies. I've read a lot of biography's, but I like to read thrillers, mysteries, and I used to like romances, but not anymore."

I saw a flash of hurt in her eyes when she mentioned romances. "I heard you were engaged to be married. I'm sorry it didn't work out." I perused a shelf on the other side of the library.

"Yes, Aunt Agatha loves to tell the story. She's just glad I'm not leaving her and can be her companion forever." She slammed the book she'd been holding onto the bookshelf.

"I'm sure she wants you to be happy, doesn't she?"

She sighed, sitting down in one of the overstuffed chairs. "I don't know. I suppose so. She was furious when I called the wedding off, but I figured that was because of all the money she'd spent."

"May I ask what exactly happened?" The look on her face told me, no, but she started talking.

"His name was Jason Wood. He was so sweet and nice. We met at a party, and we talked the whole night. I was thrilled when he asked me out. Then, when he asked me to marry him? I couldn't believe it at first, even with the ring on my finger. I was so ecstatic." She looked down at the floor. "I should have realized that wasn't in the cards for me."

I pulled up a chair, sat in front of her, and took her hands, "Everyone deserves to be happy, Doreen, especially you."

She looked up at me, "Well, if that happens, at least Margery won't be around to mess it up this time."

"What did Margery have to do with it?" I tried not to push too hard.

"Grandmum and Margery's husband, George, were good friends. When George became engaged to Margery, Gram tried to talk him out of it. Almost did, supposedly, but Margery can be very persuasive. When Margery found out I was engaged, she seduced Jason and arranged it so I'd find them together. I was still willing to marry him, but he wouldn't marry me. He said he wasn't worthy of my love. Shortly after that, he committed suicide."

My heart sunk. Margery truly was a bitch, but I didn't think even she'd go that far. She really was a horrible person.

I squeezed her hands and said, "I am so sorry. No wonder you're upset. Seeing her again brought it all back, didn't it?"

"That's not the only reason I'm upset, Molly." She looked at me, wringing her hands together.

"What else?" I let go of her hands, and she wrapped her arms around herself like she was cold.

"I think Grandma Agatha may have killed her."

Oh, my goodness, not again! I took a deep breath, "What makes you think Aunt Agatha killed her?"

She tilted her head back on the chair and said, "I went to our room after dinner because I had a horrible headache. Our room faces the garden. I was out on the balcony, getting some fresh air, and I saw Grandmum headed for the garden. What if they argued? She's very strong; she could easily have done it!"

"Do you know what time this was?"

"Not really. I came up after dinner. That was about nine o'clock, wasn't it? I took a long bath and got into my pajamas and robe. So, maybe ten?"

"Ten?"

"I think so, why?"

"Look, I don't think Aunt Agatha would do such a thing, but I'll try to find out the time frame of her death. Okay? We didn't find her until one o'clock, so maybe Aunt Agatha just told her off, and she was alive when they parted. Do you remember what time she got back to your room?"

"Around eleven, I think. I pretended I was asleep, so I didn't have to talk to her."

"Okay. I'll see what I can find out and let you know. Okay?"

"Thanks, Molly."

Right then, the gong rang for lunch, so we made our way to the dining room, forgetting all about books. I had my own mystery to solve.

I waited until lunch was over, and Aunt Agatha was on her way to her room to "digest." I followed her, catching up with her on the stairs, "How are you, Aunt Agatha? I have had little time to talk to you since you've been here."

With one hand on the banister, and one hand on her cane, there was little room for me beside her, so I stayed one step below, hoping she didn't trip and take us both out. She glanced back at me, her eyebrows arched, "Finding dead bodies all over the place leaves little time for socializing, my dear." Her flowered dress reached past her knees, but not quite long enough to cover her nylon knee-highs. She smelled of onions and lilac, not a pleasant combination.

"Yes, well, I guess not. Do you have time to talk now?" We'd reached the top of the stairs, and I was able to stand beside her.

"A few, but I really need to go lie down and digest. Why Doreen and I have to share a room is beyond my comprehension. There's plenty of room here."

Her jowls shook as she spoke, and I tried not to stare. "There was a full house, Aunt Agatha. Are you headed home, or are you planning to stay for a few more days? The detective said everyone can leave, so I'm sure you could have your own room now if you prefer."

"We're here until Thursday. Maybe I'll speak to your mum about it." As we arrived at her room, I opened the door for her. She walked in first, setting her cane down by the dresser, taking off her sweater, and hanging it on the chair. I sat down on Doreen's bed. She sat down on the other bed, facing me.

Now that I had her attention, I wasn't sure where to start. I'm sure asking her if she killed Margery probably wasn't a good place to begin. "Did you enjoy the gala?"

Like Doreen, she also wore glasses, her pair held around her neck with a gold chain. She slipped them onto her nose and picked up her book from the nightstand.

"You mean other than the cold-blooded murder that took place?" She looked at me over her glasses.

"Well, yes, that was rather inconvenient, wasn't it?" I stopped myself from rolling my eyes. "Did you, by chance, talk to Margery at all?" I watched her face for any type of reaction.

"Now, dear, what reason on earth would I have to speak to that woman?"

I looked at her pale face, other than the bright spots of red blush, she'd looked me straight in the eye. Wasn't that a sign they were telling the truth?

"Why are you asking all of these questions? I told all of this to that ridiculous man who calls himself a detective."

"I just wondered. I thought I heard someone mention they'd seen the two of you in the garden."

"Whoever said that was lying. I spent much of my time talking to that airhead of a sister of yours. Then, I ran into a friend of mine and spent the rest of the time catching up with her. Now, I really must rest if you wouldn't mind running along."

She laid down with her book as I got off Doreen's bed. I was fuming at her remark about Fiona. She was hardly an airhead. I took the light blanket lying at the foot of the bed and covered her up.

"Thank you, dear," she murmured, not taking her eyes from her book.

"You're welcome." I walked out of the room and closed the door. What was she hiding? I wonder how long it will take her to realize she was holding the book upside down.

# # #

I walked down the hall, around the corner, and went into my room, pulling my phone from my pocket and called Callum.

"Hey, Molly. I've been meaning to call. How are you?"

"I'm doing okay, but I have a question for you." I pulled my laptop out of my closet and sat on the bed.

"Ah...what kind of question?"

"Do you know, or can you find out, the time frame of when Margery died?"

He lowered his voice as he said, "I'm not on the case, remember?"

"I know, but she was your ex-wife. You would be perfectly justified in asking." I signed into the computer and pulled up my email.

He sighed. "I'll see what I can do." He disconnected the call.

Not sure if it was due to the weather or not, but the Internet was spotty, and so I was still going through my email when he texted me back thirty minutes later. I checked my phone, and there were two new messages. The first one said, "Between 11p-1a". The second one, "U O Me."

I pulled up my list of suspects and added Aunt Agnes and crossed off Mrs. Riley, so my list now looked like this:

Callum Murphy married to Margery, divorced after six months. Doesn't appear to have any feelings for her at all, let alone murderous ones. Other than the fifteen minutes at half-past nine when he saw here out, he was with me the whole night.

~~Beatrice Riley wouldn't sell the bookstore to her, didn't like her because she was a "hussy" and was an unpleasant customer. Thinks she knows who the killer is.~~

Dillon Quinn broke up with Margery, but she wouldn't accept it. Had an argument with victim before she was killed. However, that was at approximately half-past nine. Dillon then got a bottle of whiskey from Scott (need to verify).

Scott, the bartender, wasn't fond of her, but why? Because she wouldn't leave Dillon alone, or did he have a romantic history with the victim?

Jayne Webster knew George Denton, Margery, had an affair with Jack.

Jack Webster furious at Margery because she told Jayne about the affair at the gala.

Aunt Agnes Doreen saw her together with Margery at 10p. Aunt Agnes says it wasn't her. Who is lying?

The list did nothing but frustrate me. I honestly couldn't believe anyone on this list would have killed her. There was one person I forgot, though—the unnamed man in the video. Hopefully, either Fiona or Bethany would be able to identify him later. Thinking about the two of them reminded me I needed to let Mum know I was going to Fiona's for dinner. Then, I needed to beg a vehicle, stop at Fiona's office, pick up the key, and then stop at the market and pick up the ingredients for dinner. I turned off my laptop and added it to my backpack.

I took a quick shower and changed into a clean pair of jeans, added a long-sleeve tee-shirt, and a cardigan grabbed my backpack and set out to find Mum.

She was in the parlor talking to Jayne. I knocked on the door, and she looked to see who it was. "Oh, come in, dear. Jayne and I were just talking about you."

"Is that why my ears were ringing?" I smiled.

Jayne said, "It's good to see you smile, Molly. You've been through so much the past couple of days." She lifted the teacup to her lips.

"Yes, darling. You really need to stop finding dead bodies," Mum added, shaking her head.

"Mum, I didn't go out looking for them," I answered grouchily.

"Well, you know what I mean." She sipped her tea.

"Well, I came to tell you I'm having dinner at Fiona's tonight."

"Fiona's cooking?" She winced. "Are you sure that's a good idea?"

I laughed, my mood a little lighter. "No, I'm cooking. I have to stop by her office and pick up her key."

"Oh, that reminds me. One of the maids found something while cleaning her room after she left yesterday." She looked around the room. "Where did I put that?" She jumped up off the couch and went over to the fireplace mantle. "Ah, here it is." She came over and handed it to me.

Without looking at it, I stuck it in my pocket, kissed both ladies on the cheek, and said my goodbyes.

Chapter 18

I arrived at Fiona's house at half-past three, my arms filled with groceries. I unlocked the door and set the groceries on the counter. The taco casserole didn't take long to bake, so while it was in the oven, I looked around Fiona's house. The furniture in the living room was nice and brand new. I sat down on the soft cushions of the suede sofa when I spotted the bookcase across the room. I was impressed with her array of mysteries. Some I looked forward to reading myself. The walls were painted a light blue, but I couldn't help notice how empty they were. Where were all of her pictures? She had to have some. I decided to snoop through the rest of the house and see what I could find. In the spare bedroom, there was a large box with photo frames of all shapes and sizes. I sat on the floor and decided to snoop some more. There was a family picture taken at the Cliffs of Moher when we were all teenagers. Pictures of Fiona with her friends. Some I recognized, some I didn't. I looked at one with her and a man I didn't recognize. I read the date in the corner. It was taken three years ago while I was in America. I couldn't help but get melancholy over all the time I missed with my family while I was away. I was just about to dig deeper when I heard the door open, so I put them all back in the box and went out to the kitchen.

Fiona walked in, Bethany right behind her. The two were laughing, and Fiona said, "I'm so glad to be home. My boss can be such a jerk sometimes!" She dropped her purse and car keys on the table near the door and then hung up her coat. I was smiling when she turned around.

"What?" She looked down at her skirt and sweater, and then back at me, "Why are you smiling?"

I shrugged. "No reason. I'm just thrilled to be a part of your life again." I gave her a hug.

Bethany was hanging up her coat as she said, "I can't thank you enough for inviting me tonight. It's not much fun eating alone,"

"I know what you mean," Fiona added. "I often just make myself a toasty or order take away for dinner because I don't like to cook."

"Well, why don't you two relax? Fi, there is a bottle of wine chilling in the fridge. I just need to make the salad, and then dinner should be ready. I hope you like it, it's a taco casserole." I pulled open the refrigerator door and handed Fiona the wine, then pulled out the vegetables I'd purchased earlier. Then, I began pulling open cupboard doors, not finding what I was looking for, and closing them again.

"What are you looking for?" Fi asked as she pulled the cork off the wine bottle.

"A cutting board. Dare I hope you have one?"

"I'm not sure. What does it look like?" She pulled three wine glasses out of a cupboard and started pouring.

Bethany came over to the counter to get her wine and laughed. "Are you serious? You don't know what a cutting board is?"

"I don't cook! You know that! Well, at least nothing that you have to put in an oven. I'm surprised the thing works." She took a sip of her wine.

I looked at her, shaking my head. "It's a board you cut things on. Don't you ever make a salad for dinner?"

She opened up a cupboard I hadn't gotten to. "Sometimes, and when I do, I use this." She pulled out a plastic mat and handed it to me.

Both Bethany and I laughed. "That's a cutting board!" I shook my head as I placed it on the counter and started cutting up vegetables.

Dinner was a success, and they both liked the casserole. We quickly washed and dried dishes and were standing around her kitchen. "I have something I need the two of you to see."

I gathered my backpack, took out the laptop and the thumb drive, walked over to the table, and sat down. The other two did as well with their refilled wine glasses.

I booted it up and then added the thumb drive, "For mature audiences, only. Do either of you know who that is?" I turned it around so they could see it.

Fiona's eyes went wide, and Bethany's mouth opened. She looked at my sister. "Fiona, isn't that your—"

"Oh my God, that's my boss!" Fiona yelled and quickly closed the laptop, taking a long drink of her wine. She pointed to the laptop. "Where did you get that?" She pulled the thumb drive out and handed it to me. "I can never un-see that!" She sat back in her chair, laying her forehead on the table.

"Well, I put my lock picking skills to work and broke into Margery's house."

"Wait. You know how to pick a lock? Cool," said Bethany.

Fiona lifted her head slightly off the table, turning it toward Bethany. "That's what you got out of that? You didn't catch the part about breaking into Fiona's house?"

She took a sip of her wine, trying to hide a smile. She set it back down and looked at me with a frown. "Oh, you probably shouldn't have done that, Molly."

Fiona put her head back down on the table, and Bethany mouthed to me, "Can you teach me?" I nodded my head and smiled.

I patted Fi's back. "If it makes you feel better, I confessed to the cops, dear sister."

She sat up straighter. "Yes, that makes me feel better, but who did you call for bail?" She smirked.

"Ha, ha. I'll have you know, Detective Fitzgerald was pleased I'd found something his people didn't."

Bethany grinned. "A policeman was pleased someone interfered with their investigation?"

"Okay, well, not exactly pleased, but since I found something they didn't, he let me off with a warning. But that's beside the point. The point is, I found the memory stick, along with two notebooks, in the floor in Margery's apartment." I picked up my backpack and pulled out the copies I'd made and spread them out on the table.

"See these initials?" I pointed to the page where the initials of the man were on the video.

They both nodded.

"Those initials match the initials on the thumb drive." I picked it up and showed them.

"Fiona, what's your boss's name?"

"Barret Lewis. My God, he's married with two children!"

"What's the five thousand euros for?" Bethany asked. Then, her eyes went wide. "He's being blackmailed."

Fiona shook her head. "That bastard!" She got up from her chair and started pacing.

"Was he at the gala?" I took a sip of my wine.

She nodded. "I need dessert."

I looked at my watch. "I didn't even think of it, but the bakery is still open."

Since we'd been drinking, and the bakery was only a few blocks away, we decided to walk. I put the thumb drive in one pocket, grabbed some cash out of my wallet, stuck it in my pocket, and caught up with Fiona and Bethany.

They chatted about other things on our walk, the wind blowing off the sea, making it a little chill. It wasn't long before we were standing in front of the bakery, looking through the window at the queue. We walked in, my eyes scanning all of the delectable treats available. Then, my eyes caught a sign I hadn't noticed the last time I was there. Ice cream! I didn't realize she carried ice cream. I turned and said, "I want a double-dip chocolate ice cream cone!"

Bethany smiled, but Fiona grabbed my arm.

"Look at the front of the queue!"

I leaned over to look, and my eyes went wide. I looked back at him, "Isn't that—?"

"Your boss?" Bethany finished, peeking from the other side where she was standing.

"Yes—and his wife and two kids. I can't even look at him, so he'd better not say a word to me!"

"Fiona, try to find out from his wife what time they left the gala," I whispered.

The wife had a tray with two milks, two cookies, and a piece of cheesecake on it and was carrying it to a table. The man, dressed in the same jacket I'd seen him in before, but dressed in gray tailored trousers, was busy paying as the two children, a boy and a girl around Kayleigh's age, ran toward their mum who had just sat down at a table. The man turned around and stuck his wallet in the pocket of his pants when he spotted us.

"Fiona! What a surprise!" He motioned to his wife he'd be a moment. He looked at me. "You must be Fiona's sister. Molly, isn't it?"

I nodded.

He held out his hand and said, "It's nice to meet you."

Fiona snuck away and went to speak to Mrs. Lewis.

I took his hand, and we shook hands. I've been told you can tell a lot about a man by how he shakes hands. The hand of Fiona's boss was cold and clammy. "Nice to meet you too." I stepped back a little as Bethany moved up in line, looking up at Mr. Lewis. "Didn't I see you on Center Street yesterday?"

His eyes darkened. "Center Street? No, not at all." He looked toward his family. "I should probably get going."

I pulled out the thumb drive and showed it to him. "Are you sure? I thought you might be looking for this."

He grabbed for it, but I pulled it back just in time. He leaned in and practically bared his teeth. "I want that back, and I am not paying one more penny."

I tried to keep the smile on my face. "It's been lovely to meet you too."

By the time he'd walked away, and I'd stopped shaking, Fiona and Bethany had ordered, paid, and were waiting for their items.

Fiona handed me my ice cream. "Here you go."

"Thanks." I went to pull my bills out of my pocket, and she waved her hand.

"You can pay me later." We ignored the table where the Lewis family was sitting and walked into the cool breeze, making me rethink my choice of ice cream. We'd walked a block before Bethany burst out laughing. Fiona joining in.

"I cannot believe you did that!" Bethany said.

Fiona groaned. "I will probably get fired tomorrow!"

I shook my head and said, "No, you're won't. If he says anything to you, tell him I'll send it to the Ballyquicken Newspress."

"What are you going to do with it?" Bethany bit into her chocolate cookie. "Oh, this is good."

"I don't know. I'm sure the police will realize it's missing, so I'll probably end up giving it to them." I looked at Fiona. "What did the wife say?"

"According to Joanna, they received a phone call right after dinner that one of the kids was sick. They were home by ten. I asked if Barret had left at all, maybe to get medicine, and she no, they were together the whole night, taking turns taking care of him."

"I'll check the table assignments and see who else sat at their table and verify it," I took another lick of my ice cream. One thing about it being chilly out, it doesn't melt as fast.

The walk and the shock had sobered us up. We went back to Fiona's house and finished our desserts. Fiona had purchased an entire cheesecake and tried to talk me into a piece, but I was full. Bethany declined as well.

We walked into the living room and sat down. Fiona and I took the couch, and Bethany took the recliner. I could feel something pinching, and I reached into my pocket.

"I need to pay you," I went to hand her some money, but she bent down.

"You dropped something." She handed it to me.

"You two are doing remarkably well considering the past couple of days, Molly, you especially," Bethany commented.

Fiona took my other hand. "Especially with one being Mrs. Riley. You two were so close."

"I'm doing okay. It's better when I have something to do. Maybe that's why I'm so interested in the investigation." I squeezed her hand. "I'm channeling my inner Miss Marple. The problem is I'm not having much luck. If I were her, I'd have found the odd sock by now and solved the case."

"The odd sock?" Bethany asked.

"What do socks have to do with this?" Fiona asked.

Bethany and I both grinned. "It's just a term. It's something like, well, whatever this is," I opened up my hand.

"That's not a sock," Fiona said.

Bethany leaned in and took it out of my hand. "It looks like the buttons we have on our catering uniforms. It's been bent, though," she fingered it.

"Where did it come from, Molly?"

"I don't know. Mum gave it to me before I left. She said the maid found it in your room at the manor."

"In my room?" Her forehead wrinkled, then her eyes widened. "I remember now." She looked at me. "Remember when I stepped on something right after we'd found the body?" She swallowed. "I picked it up and must have taken it to my room when I went to get my sweater. I'd forgotten all about it." She took it from Margery. "I wonder who lost it," she asked as she fingered it. "I thought it was a stone. I don't even recall taking it upstairs." She handed it back to me.

I took a close look at it. The back of it was flat; the top of it bubbled out a little with the imprint of a castle. However, it was caved in a little, probably when Fiona stepped on it.

I looked at Bethany. "Do they fall off a lot?"

She nodded. "It drives us crazy. They fall off and get lost, and the owner charges us for them. It's gotten to where whenever I find them, I keep them to use when mine fall off. I can sew another one back on." She looked at me. "So, how's this the odd sock?"

I laughed. "It's not. I was just using it as an example."

Luckily, no one asked me to continue, and I stuck it in my pocket. Shortly after that, Bethany stood up and stretched. "Thanks for inviting me for dinner, but I have to get home and get some laundry done since I didn't get it done yesterday."

She went to the closet to get her coat. I stood up as well, and she came over and gave me a hug. "Thanks for cooking, Molly. It was delicious."

"Anytime. I'm not a great cook, but I do have some favorites." I smiled.

Fiona had risen as well, and we walked Fiona to the door. Bethany gave Fiona a hug as well, and we closed the door behind her.

I went to the refrigerator and took out a bottle of water. I went to the dining room table, packed up all my stuff, and then went into the living room.

"How come you don't have any of your pictures up yet?"

"Because I've never put up a picture before in my life, and the thought of bashing my fingers with a hammer doesn't appeal to me." She looked at her bare walls.

"I can help you." I looked around. I'm not sure why it was bothering me, but they were just too empty.

"Ha! You're joking, right? You're a bigger klutz than I am." She pointed to her nose.

I looked at it closer. "I meant to tell you it looks much better now. There's hardly any bruising at all."

"It feels much better, too."

"Now, about your walls. Back in the U.S., there are hooks you can get for pictures that don't leave marks on the walls. I'm not sure if you can get them anywhere around here, but I'm willing to make a trip to the hardware store to find out. They're really easy to use. How about I check it out tomorrow, and I can come help you tomorrow night?"

Right then, I received a text on my phone. I read it and said to Fiona, "It's from Callum. Detective Fitzgerald would like my presence tomorrow morning at nine at the police station."

Fi looked at me. "I wonder what, why?"

I tried not to show her how nervous it made me feel. "No idea. It will be interesting to find out."

I drove back to the house, parking the car in the garage and entering the house through the kitchen entrance. I was about to go upstairs when I heard muttering coming from the parlor. I walked in to see Mum having a conversation—with her laptop—and she was not being very nice.

"Mum! You realize it can't hear you, right?" I smiled. It was refreshing to see my normally composed Mum so flustered.

"Oh, this darn thing! All I'm trying to do is forward this attachment with all the pictures on it to the gala guests."

"Oh, good. There are some pictures I'd like to order." I walked over, sat down next to her, and looked at her email. I could see right away what she'd done.

I went to grab her laptop. "I can fix it for you."

She slapped my hand. "No. I'd like you to show me what I did or didn't do, so I learn how to do it."

I rubbed my hand. "Okay, then." I pointed to her screen. "You see where you have all of your email addresses?"

She looked at the screen. "Yes."

"You need to move those to the line that says 'To.' You have them in the subject box, so when you press send, it doesn't have anyone to send it to."

"Well, well. I thought I did that." She moved her glasses back up on her nose, and a few seconds later, she said, "Yay, it sent," and she set the laptop down on the table.

"You included me on that email, didn't you?" I sat back on the couch.

"Yes, dear, I did. Thank you for your help." She turned, tucking her legs under her. "How was dinner at Fiona's? Did you have a nice time?"

I gave her the play-by-play, excluding the run-in with Fiona's boss. I did, however, ask her, "Do you remember who the caterer was for the gala?"

"Of course. It was Castle Catering out of Ballyquicken. Why do you ask?"

"Just curious. The food was quite good. By the way, may I use your car again in the morning?"

"What time?"

"I'm not sure. I have to be at the police station at nine."

"I have a committee meeting at half-past nine in Ballyquicken, so how about I drop you off?"

"That will work. I can find a ride back."

Chapter 19

I woke up Tuesday morning to my alarm, hitting the snooze button. Why on earth would I set an alarm? I don't have to go to work. I rolled over and then groaned. Shoot, I have to be at the police station at nine, and I had some things I wanted to get done before Mum dropped me off. I pulled myself out of bed and glanced out the window to see a clear blue sky. I opened it up to hear the birds chirping and the hum of a lawnmower off in the distance. I quickly took a shower and chose to wear one of the dresses I'd purchased locally for my date with Liam. Date! I don't think a summons to the police station, especially by his sergeant, is considered a date. Regardless, I wanted to look my best, so I took my time with my makeup and even added a spritz of perfume.

I couldn't help but think about the button. Was that the odd sock? I looked up the number for Castle Catering on my phone, and there was no answer, so I left a message.

The next thing I did was open my laptop and update my suspect list. I placed Barrett Lewis at the bottom, adding, "Being blackmailed by Margery. Paid the money, but the thumb drive still at her house." Then, I wondered why. Why were they still at her house? I assumed she would receive their payment and hand them over, but what if she didn't? I only copied the last couple of pages of the notebook. What if she received multiple payments and someone got tired of paying? That would be more than enough motive to kill someone. I wonder if I can get anything out of Liam.

I pulled out my sunglasses as Mum pulled out of the driveway. "Thanks for driving me to the station."

"You're welcome. Any suggestions on what I'm to tell all of our friends and neighbors when they call asking why I dropped my daughter off at the police station?"

I laughed. "Just tell them I was corrupted when I went to America."

A few minutes later, we pulled into the station, her clock in her car saying eight-fifty-nine. I kissed her on the cheek and made my way into the station.

Callum was on the phone and greeted me with a wave. Liam must have heard me come in, as he walked out of the office a few seconds later, a smile on his face, making me glad I took extra care getting dressed.

"Feel like a field trip?"

I glanced at Callum for a hint, but he was still on the phone. "Sure. Where are we going?"

He took my arm and walked me out the door. "It's a surprise." He helped me into his Miata, and a few minutes later, we were on the highway.

"Any information on the blackmailers?"

He slipped his sunglasses on, and my heart fluttered again. "We've figured some of them out. Funny thing, though. We've matched all the thumb drives to the initials in the notebook except one. You wouldn't know anything about that, would you?" He glanced at me before looking back at the road.

I dug in my purse, then held it out to him. "You mean this one?"

He took it from my hand, a little bit of a zing going through me when he touched my fingers and stuck it in his shirt pocket.

"You didn't tell me where we're going."

"I know."

"We're headed to Ballyquicken."

"I don't suppose we're going to a car dealership. I really need to buy a car."

He grinned. "Not on the agenda for today."

I looked at him out of the corner of my eye. "Well, it's too late for breakfast and too early for lunch. You're taking me to see Sandy and her puppies?" I grinned.

He chuckled. "Maybe, if we have time."

"How many did she have?" I looked out the window, enjoying the view of the green, rolling hills.

"Six—three males, three females."

"Can I have one? Please? I'm willing to pay for it. Well, wait, how much are you going to want for it?"

"I thought your parents wouldn't allow you to have pets."

"They won't, but my intention is to find my own place." Liam took the roundabout, and we arrived in Ballyquicken. "Wow, this town has really built up since I was here last."

"How long ago was that?"

I thought about it for a second. "I'm not sure, actually. I don't think we came here when I was home three years ago, so since before I left."

"Did you keep in touch with Mrs. Riley?"

"I was so homesick at first, I wrote to everyone, but it was mostly by email. Mrs. Riley wasn't big on email, so I had to sit down and write an actual letter. I think I wrote four or five, then it turned into Christmas cards, birthday cards. I did send flowers and a letter when her husband died, but that was a few years ago." I looked at his profile. "Why are you asking?"

He pulled into a driveway of a metal and glass building, the type of buildings that keep popping up in the larger towns, overwhelming the historical buildings that had hundreds of years of history. We got out of the car, and Liam led me through the double glass doors and to the elevator. I tried to glance at the company names on the wall as we walked past, but keeping up with Liam wasn't easy. He hit the number six and was silent as he stood next to me, so I spent the time watching the floor numbers rise as they flashed on the screen above the door.

The doors opened, and he let me go first. I stopped and waited, as I had no clue where we were going. He took my arm and led me to an office down the hall and to the right. He opened up another glass door with "Winthrop and Sons Solicitors" etched onto it and walked up to the reception desk. The woman was on the phone, and as soon as she hung up, she looked at Liam and said, "May I help you?"

"We have an appointment with Mr. Winthrop. Detective Liam Fitzgerald and Molly McGuire."

"Which Mr. Winthrop? Senior or Junior?"

Liam pulled out his notebook and flipped through some pages. "Senior."

She picked up the receiver, and a few moments later, another woman came out and greeted us. "I'm Shelley Thompson, Mr. Winthrop's assistant. Come this way, please."

We walked down a hall with offices on both sides and abstract paintings on the walls that looked like ink blots that a psychiatrist would ask you about. Do you see a butterfly or an ape? I grinned to myself as she led us to a conference room at the end of the hall and asked us if we'd like any refreshments. We both declined.

I sat in the comfy swivel chair and turned to Liam. "What's this about, Liam? Why are we here?"

Before he could answer, a distinguished gentleman in his sixties in a very expensive suit walked in with a file in his hand. He came up to Liam and held out his hand. "Detective Fitzgerald, I presume?"

Liam stood up and took his hand. "Yes." He turned to me and said, "This is Molly McGuire. Thank you for seeing us on such short notice."

He and I shook hands, and he sat down across from us at the oak table. "Thank you for coming. This shouldn't take long," His hair was gray, his eyes green, and he was smiling, so I took that as a good sign.

"I'm sorry, but just who are you again?" Why did I have this sudden urge to run?

Mr. Winthrop glanced between us. "Didn't the detective tell you?" He looked at Liam. "I'm Beatrice Riley's solicitor."

I hadn't realized my body had tensed up until I felt myself relax. "It's nice to meet you. Is this about the funeral? I'd like to offer to take care of it if I can."

Mr. Winthrop shook his head, "That's all taken care of. The funeral will be on Thursday at eleven at St. Mary's. She prearranged it many years ago."

"So why am I here?" I glanced at the lawyer, then at Liam, who stayed silent.

Mr. Winthrop cleared his throat, "Mrs. McGuire, you're the sole beneficiary of Beatrice's estate."

"What? That can't be right." I sat back in my chair. "This has to be a mistake." I looked between the two of them.

"It's no mistake, Mrs. McGuire. You own the house, the bookstore plus a hefty sum of money, even after inheritance taxes."

"I can't believe this. Why me?"

"When Henry Riley died three years ago, Beatrice realized she needed to have a will. With no family, she couldn't decide who her beneficiary should be. Once I told her it didn't need to be a family member, she thought of you."

"I wasn't even living here until a week ago." I looked from Liam to Mr. Winthrop. "There has to be someone else." I felt like the room was closing in on me, and the tears began to fall. I don't know why, but all I could think of was how carefully I'd applied my makeup that morning, and it now was probably ruined.

Mr. Winthrop stood and put a box of tissues out in front of me. I took the whole box and set it in my lap. I could feel a headache starting in my left temple, and closed my eyes for a moment. Mrs. Riley, I really let you down, didn't I?

I wiped my tears, the mascara confirming my fear. I wiped my nose and looked at Mr. Winthrop. He had an envelope in his hand. He held it out to me, and I read the front. In Mrs. Riley's lovely script, it read, "Molly Quinn."

I laughed as I took it from him. "She never did like the fact I'd married a Yank." I stuck it in my purse.

"Do I have to accept it?"

"No, but why don't you let it sink in for a day or two, and we can talk later in the week. Maybe whatever's in that envelope will help you make up your mind."

I nodded, finally looking at Liam. "Do you have anything else you need to discuss with Mr. Winthrop?"

He shook his head and stood up. We both said our goodbyes and walked out. It took me a minute or two to ask myself why a detective would take the beneficiary to the solicitor's office. The answer came to me along with my gritting teeth and my clenching fists.

I kept quiet until we were outside, rushing to get a few steps ahead and then stopped, turning to face him.

"You are a lowdown, unscrupulous, snake!"

His jaw clenched. "Molly—"

"You did that on purpose! You knew I was Mrs. Riley's beneficiary, and you wanted to see how I'd react. You think I killed her!" I turned around and started walking toward the parking lot.

"Wait!" He grabbed my arm. I stopped but didn't look at him. "Can we please talk about this?"

I reluctantly turned around, and he led me to a nearby bench under a giant oak tree where we both sat down. He took a deep breath. "Okay, I admit I knew, but I needed to see your reaction."

"Yes, I figured that part out," I snapped.

"You have to understand something." He bent over his elbows on his knees, avoiding my gaze. "I am a damn good detective, known for being able to keep my emotions out of an investigation." He sat up and looked at me. "Until now. I probably should have excused myself from this investigation, but I couldn't. And I don't know what to do with you, Molly McGuire. I don't know if I should arrest you for interfering or…"

"Or?"

"Or kiss you."

My anger slightly dissipated. "I would prefer being kissing over being arrested."

He smiled, turning toward me. He took my hand in his. "Me too. However, you are a suspect in not just one, but two, homicides. I know you had nothing to do with either of them, but I needed to see your reaction. Can you understand that?"

All I could do was nod. "The murders are connected, aren't they?"

"Yes. We spoke to Beatrice's date. Beatrice wanted to see the fountain before he took her home. That was about ten o'clock. She'd kept him on the dance floor all night. He hadn't any energy left, so she went alone. When she returned, she was upset and eager to leave. He tried to get her to talk about what was bothering her, but she wouldn't tell him."

"So, she knew who the murderer was. I failed her. I should have dragged her to the police station after church."

"It's not your fault."

"Wait, you said, half-past ten?"

He nodded. "Why?

"Nothing really. I just thought of something." I smiled. I made a mental note to see what Aunt Agnes and Mrs. Riley were wearing at the gala. They're both about the same height, both with those gray pin curls. Could Mrs. Riley be who Doreen saw in the garden at ten o'clock?

"Are you okay?" He squeezed the hand he'd been holding.

His voice brought me back from my reverie. "May I ask who the beneficiary of Margery's estate is?"

"Molly…"

"Please, Liam. I promise no one will find out you told me."

He smiled. "Joshua Denton."

I gasped. "The stepson?" That caught me by surprise.

He sighed again. "Yes, the stepson. He lives in Cork and will arrive in town this afternoon." He pulled me up from the bench. "How about we go see some puppies?"

#

After dragging me away from playing with the puppies, Liam dropped me off at home. They were only a week old, their eyes not even open yet. They stayed very close to their mum, stumbling over one another, just being adorable. I fell in love with one of the females in the litter. She was the only one all golden other than white patches on her shoulders. I convinced Liam to hold her for me, and

I couldn't wait until she was old enough to come home with me. I'd taken a ton of pictures on my phone, and I couldn't wait to show them to Fiona. Before I got out of his car, Liam did ask me to think about the inheritance. I told him I would.

I returned to my room and opened my laptop. I had two more suspects to add, and then made another list deleting the names of the people I had reason to believe were innocent.

<u>Scott, the bartender,</u> need to talk to him

<u>Aunt Agnes</u> could it have been Mrs. Riley, who was seen in the garden?

<u>Barret Lewis</u> being blackmailed by Margery.

<u>Joshua Denton</u> stepson and beneficiary of Margery's estate

I left Aunt Agnes on the list for now until I verified if she and Mrs. Riley, were in fact, mistaken for one another. I looked at Joshua's name. Liam said he was in town today. I wonder if I could talk to him.

My mind wandered to Mrs. Riley. I pulled out the envelope Mr. Winthrop had given me and opened it.

Dear Molly,

If you're reading this, it means I've joined my dear Henry in God's house. Don't mourn for me. I've had a marvelous life.

You're probably wondering why I left all of my belongings to you, especially since, unless things have changed, you're living in America married to that Yank.

As you know, Henry and I were never blessed with children. In many ways, the Book Bin was our baby, watching it grow from an infant into a full-fledged adult. But the truth of the matter is, it was our employees. I think that's one of the reasons we employed young people because you brought such joys to our lives, especially you.

You were our favorite, the one we wished was ours. I love you like a daughter. Hence, I'm leaving our legacy to you.

I know this may cause some complications with you being in America, but you know your true home is here in Ireland, and I hope you will think about keeping our baby and making her your own.

All my love,

Beatrice Riley

I put the letter down, grabbed some tissues from the bathroom, and looked in the mirror. Looking at my tear-stained face, I could see my makeup had mostly disappeared, and my eyes were bloodshot. I quickly washed my face and redid my makeup, but not quite as carefully as I had that morning. I put my hair into a ponytail and went downstairs.

Mrs. Jones offered me some lunch, handing me a note from Mum, reminding me I had several boxes in the garage that required my attention. Not how I'd planned to spend the afternoon, but I headed to the garage anyway.

Chapter 20

When I returned from outside, my cheeks were rosy, and I was dying for a cup of tea. I walked into the sitting room and found Mum seated there, going through the mail. A few minutes later, Mrs. Jones brought us tea and Mum served.

"Did you receive many phone calls asking about your wayward daughter?" I took a sip of my tea.

She smiled. "I did, but only three. The village must have slept in this morning. How did your morning go? Any news on who the culprit is?"

I told her about the inheritance. She didn't seem surprised.

I added a cookie to my plate. "Did you know I would inherit?"

"No, but it doesn't surprise me. She loved you like a daughter. I used to be very jealous of her and that bookstore."

"Jealous? Why?" I took a bite of the cookie. Molasses. Yum.

"Because you thrived there. You were in your element. You've always loved books, and you would come home jabbering on about how wonderful Mr. and Mrs. Riley were."

"They were lovely people, you know. At least the one bright spot about all of this is they're now back together." I refilled my teacup. "What should I do?"

"It's your decision, dear. She adored you enough to leave the bookstore to you, which says a lot. She knows you would take care of her legacy."

I sighed. "You're right." I put my hand over hers. "Thank you."

I left mum to look up the solicitor's phone number on my laptop. Mr. Winthrop said he was glad I'd changed my mind, and we set up an appointment for later in the week.

I begged Mum's car and drove into town, driving past Margery's house, a sports car parked in the driveway. I parked in front of the house and knocked on the door.

The same man I'd seen in pictures answered the door. "Yes?"

"Josh Denton?"

"Can I help you?" His brown eyes darted past me nervously.

"I'm Molly McGuire. I wanted to offer my condolences. May I come in?"

He opened the door to let me in. "Please, sit down. You were one of those who found her, right?"

"I was. Along with a friend of mine and my sister."

"May I offer you some tea?" He sat in the chair across from me, then popped back up like a Jack-in-the-box.

"No, thank you." I looked at him and asked, "May I ask when the funeral will be?"

"The police haven't released her body yet, so hopefully the end of the week." He was fidgety. "I appreciate you stopping by. My step-mum wasn't all that well-liked."

"I must admit she wasn't one of my favorite people either, but she didn't deserve to die that way. Do you have any idea who would do this to her?"

He shook his head. "I haven't seen her in a few years. I'm very surprised to find out I'm her beneficiary. I didn't realize she had no one else."

"You liked her." Although I found it hard to believe anyone would.

"I did. Most people thought she was after my dad's money. If you paid attention, you could see there was real love there."

"You have a sister, I believe?"

"Yes, Elizabeth. The last I heard from her she was in Australia. She hated Margery."

"Did they not get along?" I asked.

"They never actually met, believe it or not. I think Elizabeth just didn't like the thought of anyone taking our mum's place. The two of them were very close."

"Really, they never met?" Then, why so much anger and hatred?

"Not once. Dad had convinced her to come home, and then shortly after that, he passed away. Elizabeth was convinced Margery had killed him."

"What do you think?"

"It's bullocks, of course. He died of a heart attack."

"I'm sorry to hear that. And you're sure you have no idea where she is?"

He shook his head. "I haven't even spoken to her in over a year."

"Have you thought of hiring a private detective to find your sister?"

"I've thought about it. I can afford it. Other than a stipend left to Margery, our dad left his fortune to me and Elizabeth."

"Margery always implied he'd left her the bulk of the money."

"No. She ended up with about ten thousand euros was all."

So, that explains the blackmail. She had to do something to keep up her standard of living.

"Where are you living now?"

"Cork, where I grew up. I own a couple dealerships, one in Cork and one in Ballyquicken."

"A car dealership? I'll have to come see you. I'm in the market for a car myself."

He pulled out his wallet and handed me a card. "Please do. Although what you're driving now is nice."

I laughed. "It's my mum's. I just moved back to Dooley a little over a week ago."

"I'll give you a good deal. Please, give me a call." He grinned.

"Do you have a wife? Children?"

"Not yet. I'm hoping someday." He grinned. He had a really nice smile.

"Have you ever been to Dooley before?" I couldn't help but wonder if he murdered Margery for the inheritance. Ironic, isn't it? Liam thought the same about me.

"No. This is my first time. It seems like a decent place. Where would you suggest for a quick, easy dinner? A bonus if it has great pie."

"Dooley's Café has decent food and great pie. You're a man after my own heart." I tucked my hair behind my ear and gave him my best smile. "You weren't here on Saturday, then, by chance?"

He returned it. "No, I was at a friend's house taking part in a very intense poker game. Just why are you asking, Ms. McGuire?"

"Just curious. Thank you for your time, Mr. Denton." I looked at the business card. "I will be visiting you soon."

Damn! I was really hoping he was a viable suspect. Too bad the sister isn't anywhere near Dooley. She'd be the prime suspect for sure.

I left Center Street, drove back into town, and pulled into the pub parking lot, hoping Scott was working. I got to the door just in time to see two constables haul Dillon into a police car. I ran into the pub. I didn't even have to ask Scott. He just pointed. "He's in his office."

Aiden had the phone to his ear. "Thanks, Dad. I'll meet you there."

His face looked panicked. "How did you hear so fast?"

"I didn't hear. I saw the police haul him away." My stomach clenched at the thought of Dillon in jail.

"I just spoke to Dad. He's calling Jack Webster, but it will take him at least two hours to get here. I'm headed over there now. Do you want to come with me?"

"I'll meet you there. May I use your desk for a few minutes?"

He nodded. I heard him tell Scott he was in charge, and all was quiet. I pulled open the drawers of the desk until I found a notepad and a pen. I left the office and moved to the bar. "Scott, may I have a ginger beer, please?"

Scott took a glass from under the bar and filled it with ice, setting it in front of me. He turned around and grabbed a bottle from the refrigerator behind him. He opened the top and set it beside the glass. "I can't believe they arrested Dillon. He wouldn't kill Margery. If he killed every woman he broke up with, half of Dooley's female population would be dead."

"Why didn't you like Margery?"

He poured my drink and set it in front of me. "I didn't like the way she treated people."

"Did you ever date her?"

"I'm gay, Molly, so no. She's not my type."

"Oh, well, that would make a difference, wouldn't it?" I cleared my throat to try to hide my embarrassment.

He smiled and nodded at my blank notebook. "What are you doing?"

"Trying to figure out who killed her. I have to be missing something."

"Who are your suspects?"

"There is myself, my sister Fiona, Fiona's boss, Callum, Dillon, my Aunt Agnes, her granddaughter Doreen, Josh, who is Margery's stepson, and Elizabeth, the stepdaughter who no one has heard from in over a year."

He leaned against the bar with a towel over his shoulder. "I'm assuming you didn't do it, or your sister. I could see leaving Callum on the list. She's his ex-wife. But why would he wait four years to do it? Dillon wouldn't do it either. Do you really think your aunt or cousin did it?"

"No. My aunt has an alibi, and Doreen wouldn't have the strength to lift her into the fountain."

"What about your sister's boss?" he asked.

"I don't think so. According to his wife, they left the gala early because their son was sick."

"What do you know about the stepson?" He started wiping off the counter.

"I just came from talking to him. I don't think he did it. He inherited, but it came as a surprise. He hadn't seen Margery in over a year. Plus, he doesn't appear to need money. He drives a fancy sports car and owns two car dealerships."

"So, that leaves the sister."

"Yes, but she's not here! The last anyone knew, she was living in Australia."

"Well, maybe she's here, but you just don't know who she is."

"Maybe. I really think it has something to do with the odd sock."

He smiled. "The what?"

"The odd sock. It's a term used in some mystery stories. Something out of place." ☐

"So, what's your 'odd sock' here?"

"The button. It has to mean something. I just don't know what."

My phone buzzed, and I read the text. It was from Callum. "I'm so sorry."

I texted back, "Take care of him. Okay?"

He returned a smiley face. I looked at Scott. "Text from Callum about Dillon."

"What is this about a button?" Scott asked.

Before I could answer, a group of six women came in and stood by the door, their arms full of shopping bags.

"You can sit anywhere you'd like, ladies." Scott smiled at them as he grabbed some menus and walked over to their table.

I checked Google for the address of Castle Catering. Thankfully, they had a location here in Dooley. I called the number, but it went to voicemail. I left a second message and hoped they would call me back.

Scott was back behind the bar getting the drinks for the table of ladies. "Were you working for Castle Catering at the gala?"

He shook his head, "Aiden and Dillon hired me, why?"

"Do you ever work events for them?" I munched on a bowl of pretzels he'd set in front of me.

"I try to stay away from catering jobs if I can. I prefer to just pick up extra shifts here."

"Did you recognize any of the catering staff working that night?"

"A few of them, but I wouldn't know their names."

"I'm trying to get a hold of the catering manager, but she's not returning my calls."

"Does this have to do with your 'odd sock' that's really a button?" He laughed.

"It does, yes." I smiled, then felt guilty with Dillon sitting in a jail cell. My phone dinged with another text message, this time from Fiona asking if I'd found the hooks for the pictures. Shoot! I'd totally forgotten about them. She must not know about Dillon, and I didn't want to bother her at work. There isn't anything we can do for him. It's all up to Jack Webster.

I paid Scott for my soda and made my way to the hardware store. I had no problem finding the hooks I was looking for, so I texted Fiona letting her know. We decided I would come to her place at half-past six. I drove to the police station.

Aiden was in the lobby. He stood up when he saw me, sweeping me up in a hug. "Any news?" I asked. Callum was behind the counter at his desk, but got up and joined us.

"They're still processing him. It will be at least another ten minutes." Callum said.

Liam, along with his sometime partner, Gary, came through a secured door at the back of the room. Callum scurried back through the gate and to his desk while I gave a scowl my mum would be proud of. Liam started to say something, but Gary cut him off.

"Molly, I'm sorry about this. We're getting pressure from above to solve this, and Dillon is our best suspect."

I crossed my arms in front of me, my fingers clenching my arms, "I thought the two murders were connected. Is that no longer the case?"

"We are investigating them as separate murders that may have a connection, yes," Gary said.

Aiden looked at the detectives nastily, "It's because Dillon has an alibi for Mrs. Riley's death. He was at the bar working."

Liam and Gary looked at each other but didn't comment. I tried to keep the anger at bay, but I could feel my face getting red. I hated feeling like this, but it was my brother damn it.

Just then, my phone rang. I excused myself to take the call. "Hello. Is this Molly McGuire. This is Betty O'Leary from Castle Catering," The woman's voice was very pleasant, helping to take my anger down a notch.

"Yes, it is. Thank you for calling me back. I'm inquiring about the staff hired for the gala at the Quinn residence on Saturday night."

"That's what your message said. Just what do you need to know?"

"I'm wondering if any of the staff turned in a jacket missing a button."

"Excuse me? A button?"

"I know it sounds strange, but can you check for me? I know this sounds like a cliché, but a life could depend on it."

"I can try, but not everyone turns them in. May I call you back?"

"Thank you." It almost came out as a growl. I feel like I'm getting close, but am still missing something. Back in the police station, Callum was the only one still there.

"Where did everyone go?" Callum stood up, came over, and opened the gate to let me in.

"Aiden is back with Dillon. The detectives gave him five minutes, so you might want to hurry."

I'd never been past the front office of the police station. Callum led me to the secure door Liam and Gary had come through earlier. A policeman seated on the other side buzzed us in. Once we were through the first door, he buzzed open the second door. We walked through to a hallway with several closed doors on each side. Callum opened the first door on the left and motioned me in.

The room encompassed everything I thought an interrogation room would look like: a laminate table in the middle with two chairs on each side, Dillon on one side, Aiden on the other. I rushed over to give Dillon a hug. He stood up as I flew into his arms.

"Please don't touch the inmate," said a voice from the corner. I turned to see Constable Mills standing there. Callum gave him a look and said, "It's okay, Mills."

"Miss Molly, I didn't realize it was you. Go ahead and hug all you want," he smiled.

I couldn't help but smile at his goofy face. "Thank you." I sat down next to Aiden, grabbing one of Dillon's hands. "Are you okay? Is there anything we can get you?"

"A cake with a file in it, maybe?" He smiled.

"I think that only works in the movies or on the telly. How about I go to the bakery and buy you a piece of cheesecake."

"No, please don't tell Reanna I'm here." The look on his face when he said her name made me think maybe Aiden was right. She was the one who got away.

"A piece of pie from the café?"

"I think I'm good. I'm sure when Jack gets here, he'll straighten this all out."

Aiden looked at him. "You're awfully cheery for a man sitting in a police station."

"Well, at least I'll get a day or two off from working at the pub." He smiled. He and Aiden shared a look I'm sure only twins could understand.

Callum cleared his throat. "I'm sorry, but times up."

We both gave our brother a hug and walked out, not stopping until we were out of the station. "I can't believe they arrested Dillon for this. I told him Margery was bad news but did he listen?" Aiden ran his hand over the back of his neck.

"It will all get straightened out." I looked at my watch. "I'd better get home and try to calm Mum down. I'm sure dads told her, and she's anxious. She can't go anywhere because I have her car." I kissed him on the cheek and went to the car, texting Mum I'd be home shortly.

Before I headed home, I thought I'd stop at the café and pick up a pie to take to Fiona's tonight. I left my car at the station and walked, slipping my sunglasses on. I could feel the heat of the sun through my blouse warming me up, which was funny since I hadn't realized I was chilled.

I cut through a parking lot and came upon the back of the café when I saw two people arguing. I didn't want to interrupt, so started back toward the sidewalk when I saw one was Josh. Who would he be arguing with? I looked closer at the second person. It was Bethany. How strange.

I bought a cherry pie and walked back to my car and drove home. Mum yelled at me the moment Higgins let me in the front door.

Chapter 21

"Where have you been? They've arrested Dillon. I have to go to him."

I sat the cherry pie on the table and pulled her into the sitting room. Mrs. Jones was bringing in a tea try, Higgins close behind.

"You are a godsend, Mrs. Jones." I poured Mum a cup of tea and handed it to her as we both sat down. Mrs. Jones and Higgins went to leave. I looked at them. "No, please stay." I poured myself a cup and sat down as well.

"I just came from the police station. Dillon is fine. I think he's much calmer than Aiden and I were." I looked at my watch. "Jack and Dad should be there soon, and I'm sure they'll take care of this, and Dillon will be out soon."

Mrs. Jones nodded. She and Higgins walked out of the room.

Mum sat on the edge of her chair. "I knew that woman was nothing but trouble. She was a devil when she was a child, and she never changed. I wished I'd have killed her myself."

"Mum! I can't believe you'd say such a thing."

"I don't mean it, Molly. It's just so darn frustrating." She sat back and took another sip of her tea.

"I know. I've been trying to figure out who did this, but I realize now I'm no Miss Marple."

"I thought you were Nancy Drew?" She was smiling

"I'm too old. I feel much more like Miss Marple these days, and a failing one at that."

"Too bad. Doesn't she always solve the mystery?"

"She does." I took a sip of my tea. "Has anyone told Fiona about Dillon?"

"Not yet. She was so upset about finding the body I didn't want to tell her at work. I'll wait until she gets off work."

My phone rang. I excused myself and took the call. It was the catering company with bad news. They didn't have any uniforms with missing buttons turned in. "We have a handful who are working an event at Dooley Castle over the weekend who kept their uniforms. Maybe one of those?"

I gave her my email address. She said she'd email me the names, so I ran upstairs, grabbed my laptop, and booted it up. I opened my email. It has been a few days since I'd checked it, and my mailbox was full. I briefly glanced through them, stopping at the email Mum sent of the gala pictures. I opened up the attachment, but there were over three-hundred photos, and it took forever for them to download. I needed to go someplace with better Internet. I shut off the computer and stuck it in my backpack. My bedside clock said it was almost half-past four, so I ran downstairs.

"Mum, I told Fiona I would go help her hang pictures at half-past six. Do you want to go with me now? We can break the news to her, and then hang pictures to keep our minds off it until we hear from Dad."

"That sounds like a great idea. I'll get my purse and meet you in the car."

I grabbed the pie off the table in the foyer and walked out to the car. Mum joined me, and a short time later, we pulled into Fiona's driveway and parked behind her Mini Cooper.

"What are you doing here already?" Then, she saw Mum behind me, her eyes wide. "What's wrong?" She opened the door wider, and we walked in. I laid the pie and the bag of hooks on her kitchen counter. Mum had taken

Fi's hand, leading her to the couch. "Honey, come sit down."

"What's going on?" She looked from me to Mum and back to me again. Mum looked like she was about to cry, so I took over.

"The police have arrested Dillon for Margery's murder."

"No! Why would they do that? He would never…"

Mum held onto her hand. "We know that, Fi. It's just taking the police a little longer to realize it."

Tears started to fall, so I added, "Dad and Jack Webster will take care of things. I'm sure we'll receive a phone call shortly telling us they're all at the bar celebrating and everything's fine."

I left her under Mum's care, as I pulled out my laptop and turned it on. I asked Fiona for her Wi-Fi password and opened my email. The photo attachment still took a few minutes to download, but much faster than previously. I began scanning the photos. "Conor West takes wonderful photos. Too bad he's such a twit when he opens his mouth."

"What are you doing?" Mum asked me.

"Looking for pictures of a member of the catering staff who is missing a button on their jacket," I said.

They both stood and moved behind me at the kitchen table. "You're right. He takes lovely pictures. Look, there's a nice one of your grandparents. I'd like a copy of that one." I made a note of the photo number but continued through them. There was a great picture of Fiona and Bethany, who I noticed had all the buttons on her jacket that Fiona said she'd like a copy of, so I added it to the list. I was almost to the end when I came across the pictures Conor had taken of me, Fiona and Callum. I noted those as well. Then, we decided to take a break.

Mum walked away, straightening her back. "Didn't you say there were pictures to be hung?"

I got up and showed them how the hooks worked. After they finished gushing about how wonderful picture hangers were, the two of them went to work going through all of the photos Fiona wanted to hang. They laid the pictures on the couch, coffee table, and floor to get an idea of what there was, making a comment she had more pictures than living room wall space. They were discussing where else they could hang them when I went back to the computer to continue looking at photos.

An hour later, we decided to take a break and order take away, although no one seemed to have much of an appetite. I had scrolled through over two hundred fifty photos before I found the pictures Conor had taken of the catering staff later in the evening. I flipped through them and found two jackets with buttons missing. One was a man in his twenties with his sandy-colored hair pulled back into a ponytail, the other was…Bethany.

"Molly, come look at the pictures we chose. Mum is superb at this."

Why wouldn't Bethany have mentioned she'd lost a button on her uniform? Did she not notice? She must not have noticed. She probably won't notice until she washes it and we'll all have a laugh about it. So, who is the man with the ponytail?

I looked over at the two of them, both standing there admiring the wall. "I will, but can you two come here and see if you have any idea who this man is?" I turned the laptop around as they approached the table. "The guy with the ponytail."

Mum went to get her reading glasses out of her purse while Fiona looked at the screen. "I don't recognize him. Bethany has mentioned she sometimes works with people who work in Ballyquicken. Maybe he's from there?"

Mum approached the table and glanced at the screen. "Now, who are we talking about?" Fiona pointed him out to her. "No idea, dear. Maybe Bethany knows." She took her glasses off and returned to the living room.

Fiona pulled her phone off the counter, and a few seconds later said, "She's not answering. That's strange. She isn't working tonight." Using her phone, she took a picture of my screen. "I'll text her the picture and ask her if she can tell us his name."

"Thanks, Fi. Where does she live?"

"She's renting a flat off High Street, right down the road from the café. Why?"

"Just curious. I'd just really like to know who this guy is," and maybe take a look at her jacket, I thought.

Mum stood looking over the pictures still on the table and floor, glancing at the wall opposite the one they just finished, as she said, "There is no reason to go over there now. I'm sure she'll get in touch with Fiona soon."

"True. So, let me see the Great Wall by Quinn." I smiled at my quip. Fiona just rolled her eyes.

There were two rows of pictures tacked up, corner to corner, set gradually by size, the larger ones on top. "This looks fabulous. Mum, will you come help me when I'm ready to decorate my home?"

"What home?" Fiona asked. "Have you purchased a house in the past twenty-four hours since we've seen each other?"

"Not exactly," I answered. Mum explained how Mrs. Riley left her inheritance to Molly.

"Molly, that's great! That explains why she was so excited about you moving home." She gave me a hug.

"Oh, and don't let me forget to show you the puppy pictures!"

I looked at the pictures, not yet hung up. I perused them where they lay until I came to a picture of Fiona and Callum. I picked that one up. They had their arms around each other. I smiled. Maybe there's a romance lurking there. "When was this taken, Fi?" I turned it around so she could see it.

"St. Patrick's Day, I think." She came closer. "It was so crowded. Bethany went home and changed into a tank top. There she is. Her back is to us. She's at the bar flirting with Scott." She pointed to a woman in a racerback tank top sporting a unicorn tattoo on her shoulder!

It felt like I'd been hit in the head with a soccer ball. It all made sense now. Elizabeth, Bethany—they both came from Cork. No one had heard from Elizabeth in the past year since she left Australia. It's because she's living here in Dooley under the name of Bethany Clark. She hated Margery. She didn't overhear me tell about Mrs. Riley seeing the murderer; I told her! The argument with Josh: Did he know she was here? Were they in on it together? I started pacing. I had to be mistaken. I sat back down at the table and pulled up my suspect list. I hadn't yet updated the list with the information Scott and I had discussed, but I did that now, and Elizabeth being the murderer was the only explanation. I wanted to be wrong. I looked at my sister. This will devastate her. I needed to speak to Bethany without Fiona or Mum knowing.

I texted Callum:

"R U @ office?"

"Y"

"Address for Bethany Clarke?"

"Who?"

"Bethany Clarke, catering staff for the gala."

"Why?"

"It's critical. Please."

I waited for a few minutes and was just about to call him when he texted back.

"1472 Castle Road, 2B."

I texted back, "Meet me there! She killed Margery and Mrs. Riley." I checked the map app on my phone to check directions on where to go and stuck the phone in my pocket.

"Hey, you two, I need some exercise after that pie. I'm going for a walk. I'll be back soon." I headed for the door.

"We haven't had pie yet, Molly," Mum pointed out.

"Wait. We'll go with you!" Fiona shouted.

I pretended I didn't hear them and shut the door. I headed down the street toward Bethany's house, my hands wrapped around my chest, trying to ward off the cool, strong breeze coming off the ocean. I started to shiver and was just about to pull out my phone to check directions when I turned the corner, and Dooley Castle came into view. It took my breath away. There were lights around it shining upward, giving the castle an eerier glow. The restored castle, as it stands today, is open to tourists, as well as renting out their luxurious rooms for events. Its tall turrets, high above the town, stood guard over the Atlantic Ocean and protected us from now nonexistent enemies. I located the building of flats next to the castle, walked up to the door, and tried to open it, but the door wouldn't budge. I tried a trick used all over the world. I started hitting buttons until someone buzzed me in. I got in on the third try.

I saw a door marked "stairs," so I opened the door and ran up the steps. If I continued visiting Reanna's bakery and eating pie from the café, I needed to exercise. I was out of breath by the time I opened the door to the second floor. I found Bethany's flat and knocked on the door.

The door opened to show Bethany in her bathrobe, her hair in a towel. No wonder she didn't answer her phone. "Molly, my goodness, what are you doing here?" She looked behind me, but then opened her door to let me in. "I just saw that Fiona called, as well as texting a picture. I just texted her back, telling her he was new, so I don't know him well. I think his name is Mike Sullivan."

I stood at the door to catch my breath. The apartment was compact. The door led into the carpeted living room with the dining room to the left, its floor laminated. She'd placed a small table with mismatched chairs in the dining room. There was a half wall between the living room and the kitchen, an overstuffed couch sitting in front of the wall. I could see a kitchen knife set sitting next to the stove and couldn't help but wonder if a knife was missing.

"Thanks. May I have a glass of water?" I asked, sitting down on her sofa. There was a coffee table sitting there, and as much as I wanted to set my feet on it, I figured a little more decorum was called for.

"Sure." I heard the tap run, and she handed me a glass with ice in it. I prayed she hadn't poisoned it as I gulped it down.

"Are you okay?" She smiled.

"I'm fine. I didn't mean to barge in on you. Are you working tonight?"

"Yes. It was supposed to be my night off, but someone went home sick, so they asked me to come in and cover the rest of her shift. Do you mind if I go get dressed?"

"Not at all. Go ahead." She turned around and disappeared.

I could still hear her, though, as she yelled, "You should stop by the restaurant sometime for dinner. The food is excellent."

I made my way into the kitchen as I yelled back. "Sounds great. Maybe the three of us can go one night."

I put my glass in the sink and looked at her knife set. There was one knife missing. I looked around the spotless kitchen and didn't see one lying around, and there was no dishwasher. I pulled out my phone and took a picture, sending it to Callum.

Turning around, Bethany was standing there. "What are you doing?"

"Me? Nothing. I was just taking a picture of your spotless kitchen. I've never seen one so clean." I stammered. "As a matter of fact, your entire apartment, I mean, flat, is spotless. You must spend a lot of time cleaning."

She had gotten dressed but was rubbing her hair with the towel previously covering it. I could see the blonde roots. Another sign she was Elizabeth.

She nodded and turned around, walking toward the coffee table sitting in front of the couch. She opened a drawer and pulled something out. Turning around, she pointed a gun at me, throwing the towel on the table.

My mouth was as dry as a desert when I went to swallow. I croaked out the words, "Bethany, what are you doing?"

"How long have you known?" Her wet hair was long and stringy, the tips leaving marks on her blouse.

I tried to answer, but all I could see was the long cylinder where a bullet could be pumped out at the touch of her very shaky finger. "Known what?" I squeaked out.

A low-pitched sound came out of her mouth, something between an evil laugh and a growl. "I had the perfect plan." She looked at me and said, "It was the damn button, wasn't it?"

All I could do was nod.

"I didn't think I'd convinced you the button had nothing to do with the murder."

"Why, Mrs. Riley? She was just a sweet old lady." I wished she would quit pointing the gun at me. How could I tell if the safety was on? I'm sure Miss Marple would know.

"I was leaving when I noticed the button had fallen off in the struggle with that bitch. I heard someone coming, so I had to stop searching. I didn't think they'd seen me, but I found out differently at the church. I didn't want to kill her, but she shouldn't have been so nosy."

"Where did you hide the knife?"

"In your garden! The day I pretended to lose my keys. It was so easy," she rolled her eyes.

"I saw you with Josh. Was he in on this too?" Where on earth was Callum?

"My dear big brother, Margery had him wrapped around her finger. Did he tell you they had an affair behind my dad's back?" She paced, but unfortunately, parallel to me so she could keep me in her gun sights. "I couldn't believe it when he showed up at the café for a piece of cherry pie. It always was our favorite. I think he was more shocked than I was when we figured it out."

I had my eye on the towel sitting on the table as she continued to pace. There were footsteps outside her door. I prayed they were the cops and not a neighbor.

"Police! Open up!" As Bethany looked toward the door, I grabbed the towel off the table, threw it over her head, and dove into her, both of us crashing to the floor, the echo of a gunshot ringing in my ears and a searing pain in my right arm. Somehow, I ended up on top of her, the gun beside me. I put my hands on her arms and lifted them over her head. The blood dripped off my arm and onto the worn carpet. There was more banging at the door, and it finally burst open. The two detectives rushed in with their guns drawn, and Callum with his baton.

"Don't move!"

I rolled off Bethany, and something stabbed into my back. I dug under my back with my left hand, pulling out the gun and holding it up in the air. "Here's the gun. And nice timing." Then, everything went black.

Chapter 22

I woke up to a blurred vision of a woman leaning over me, and a tightness around my upper left arm. The pressure released, and I heard someone say, "It's one-ten over eighty, doctor."

My head felt like it was filled with cotton candy, and as much as I wanted to ask where I was, my eyes refused to stay open.

The next time I awoke, the room was dark other than a small light beside my bed, where I could see the silhouette of someone sitting in a chair.

"Who's there?" The cotton candy had moved from my brain to my mouth. "Water?"

Whoever it was jumped from their chair, and a few seconds later, stuck a straw in my mouth. I sucked, the coolness of the water moistening my mouth. I could see the person clearly now. It was Callum.

"What are you doing here?" He was dressed in casual clothes, so he must not be here to arrest me. Wait. Should I be arrested? He was smiling, so I hoped not.

"Hey, you. How are you feeling?"

"I'm not sure. Where am I?" This didn't look like my room at home, and what are all those beeping sounds?

"You're in the hospital. You were shot, remember?"

Shot? I was shot? Oh…Bethany.

"Is Fiona mad at me?" He turned around; a scraping noise filled the room, and then he sat down and took my hand.

"Why would Fiona be mad at you?" His green eyes were scanning my face, probably thinking how awful I looked.

"Bethany was her friend."

He grinned. "But you're her big sister. I think she's more worried about you."

"What time is it?" I tried to look out the window, but the blinds had been closed.

Callum looked at his watch, "It's a little after midnight."

"That's all? I thought it would be later than that."

He smiled. "It's after midnight a day after you were shot. You've had us all worried."

"Really?"

"Yes, really. I need to let the nurse know you're awake."

"Okay. I'll just close my eyes for a minute."

The next thing I heard was a multitude of voices. Whoa, who decided my room was a good place to have a party?

I opened my eyes to a much brighter room. I turned my head. Someone had opened the blinds, and I could see flowers on a table across the room. There was also a teddy bear and a huge bouquet of—

"Balloons," I said, smiling.

"All of the voices stopped. I looked around the room to see almost my entire family, minus the kids.

"Hey there, kitten," my dad swooped in and kissed my forehead. Mum went on the other side of the bed and kissed my cheek. Ciara leaned in and set the teddy bear near my head. The teddy bear and the balloons are from the twins and Kayleigh." She smiled. "Well, mostly Kayleigh. They thought the balloons and Fred would cheer you up."

"Fred?" I know I had mashed potato brain, but who is Fred?

"The teddy bear." She had tears in her eyes.

"Don't cry. Tell her I love them both!"

Ciara wiped them away. "You eejit, that's not why I'm crying. I'm just glad you're okay."

Aiden came to her side. "You scared us, sis."

The doctor came in and shooed everyone out so he could have a look at me. He was around my dad's age, gray hair, and wore glasses. It hurt when the nurse took the bandage off, but the doctor looked at it and said it was healing nicely. The nurse rebandaged it and asked if I'd like some food.

"Yes, please."

After she left, Dillon came in, along with Reanna, who had her signature yellow box in her hands with the large R in a circle on it. I smiled when I saw them both. "Dillon, I'm so glad you're out of jail!"

He bent down and gave me a kiss on the cheek. "Me too. I can't thank you enough, sis. What you did—"

"I did because you're my brother, and I love you. I knew there was no way you would have killed Margery, no matter how much you might have wanted to. The getting shot part wasn't part of the plan, and now I get to hold it over you for the rest of your life." I grinned.

He smiled, and Reanna laughed, opening the box and showing me what was inside.

My eyes widened, "For me?" I dug in and grabbed a cookie with my left hand. The double chocolate chip cookie melted in my mouth, and I didn't realize how hungry I was.

Reanna grinned and looked at Dillon. "I told you cookies are always better than flowers."

I swallowed. "Listen to her on that one. Cookies are always better." Then, I looked at the table of goodies. "And balloons, those are from Kayleigh." I smiled, thinking of her cute little face.

Dillon took the box from Reanna, but before he could, I grabbed another cookie. He set it over on the table as Reanna took my hand.

I looked at her and whispered, "Are you two together?"

She leaned down close to my ear. "I'm not sure yet." Then, in a louder voice, she said, "I'm so glad you're okay. Don't you ever do that again!"

"I didn't plan on doing it this time. The doctor said everything is healing nicely, so I'm sure I'll be up and about soon." Dillon came back and stood beside Reanna. "Is Fiona here?"

"Of course, she is," Reanna replied. "She's just waiting to take her turn. Your mum made us draw straws."

"Like when we were kids?" I laughed. "That sounds like Mum. Always the diplomat."

Just then, Fiona burst in, "Okay, you two, my turn."

Dillon kissed my cheek, Reanna squeezed my hand, and they both left. Fiona stood in the middle of the room, dark circles under her bloodshot eyes, a foam cup in one hand, a straw sticking out, and a suitcase in her other hand. She handed me the drink, and I took a long sip. Then, she set it on the table next to me.

"You're not running away to join the circus, like when you were six, are you?" I asked with a grin.

She burst into tears and said, "Molly, I'm so sorry!" She dropped the suitcase and flung her upper half onto the bed, jolting my arm.

"Ow!"

She lifted her head and looked at my face and then at the arm that was in a sling. "Oh, my gosh, did I hurt you?"

"It's okay. I'm sure that didn't hurt as much as my hitting your nose." I smiled.

"That's probably true, but I'm sorry for that too."

"Fiona, you have nothing to be sorry about. I'm the one who owes you an apology."

"What do you have to be sorry for?" Fiona stood up.

"For proving it was Bethany. I didn't want it to be her. Well, I wanted it to be Elizabeth. I just didn't figure out Bethany and Elizabeth were the same person." I looked at her. "Now, what are you sorry for?"

"For bringing Bethany, or whatever her name is, into our lives to begin with."

"She seemed like a really nice person, well, when she wasn't killing people." I yawned.

"You're tired, but if you're up for it, you have two more visitors."

"Who is it?"

She picked up the suitcase and laid it on the end of the bed, opening it up and taking out a hairbrush. Coming over, she started brushing my hair.

"Two fine looking detectives, one with a much more worried look in his eyes than the other one."

Fiona finished my hair, added some lipstick to my lips, and gave me a breath mint. She put everything back in the suitcase. "There are some other necessities in there as well," she said as she set it down next to the flower table.

"I'll be right out here," she said as she left.

I laid my head back down on the pillow, surprised at how tired I was, but I smiled as Liam and Gary walked into the room.

"My two favorite detectives."

Gary smiled, but Liam took a look at my bandaged arm, and his jaw tensed.

"How are you, Mrs. McGuire?" Gary asked.

"Oh, please. After all of this, can't you call me Molly?" I looked into his smiling face.

He pulled up a chair and asked, "May I?"

"Of course."

Before he sat down, he took the other chair and moved it to the other side of his and looked at Liam.

"Sit."

Liam scowled at him, but he sat. I tried to hide my grin, but I think I failed because he scowled even more, crossing his arms in front of him as Gary took out his notebook.

"So, Molly, the last we saw of you, you excused yourself to take a phone call at the police station. The next time we saw you, you were passed out at the flat of one Bethany Clark, AKA, Elizabeth Denton, after being shot. Can you fill us in on how you figured out Bethany was our killer?"

I smiled. "It was the odd sock."

"The odd sock?"

"The item everyone disregards as unimportant until it is."

"Okay, but what item are we talking about?"

The button.

Liam spoke up for the first time. "What button?"

"May I have a drink, please?" I motioned to the cup on the table. Gary picked it up and handed it to me. I took it in my left hand and took a long drink. I took a deep breath and told them how I found the photos at Margery's house, how we came upon the button, the photos that Colin West took at the gala, and the identical tattoo belonging to Elizabeth Denton and Bethany Clark, and finally, the missing knife.

"It was speaking to Scott, the bartender at the pub, that made me wonder if Elizabeth was here, and then after speaking to Joshua Denton, she was the only person who hated Margery enough to kill her."

"Why didn't you call us instead of heading over there?" Liam asked.

His eyes met mine as I said, "I texted Callum, and to be honest, I don't know why I went there. I guess just instinct."

Gary took a look at Liam's face and stood up, his eyes falling on the box of goodies. "Oh, are those from Reanna's bakery?" He pointed to the box.

"Yes, please help yourself."

"I think I might just go get a cup of coffee and try one of those cookies." He went to the box, grabbed a cookie, and backed out of the room.

Liam had stood up too and moved to the left side of the bed, his hands holding tight to the rail, his knuckles white. Once again, his eyes glared at the bandage on my arm.

"Liam?" I brought my hand up to cover his.

He turned his hand around, so it was holding mine. It reminded me of when we met on the plane.

I looked into his eyes.

"Don't—you—ever—do—that—again."

I chuckled, and his hand tightened on mine.

"It's not funny, Molly." His jaw relaxed slightly, but he was still looking very disturbed.

"I know it's not. I'm sorry, but if you could see your face." I stopped chuckling and cleared my throat. "I'm okay, Liam—truly. My arm hurts like hell, but I'll be fine."

"Your arm hurts. Let me get the nurse." He went to walk away, but I didn't let go of his hand.

"I'm okay for now. I'm sure they'll give me some pain meds soon." He came to stand back by my side.

He looked into my eyes. "You scared me to death, Molly."

"Is this when you either arrest me or kiss me?" I asked, smiling.

THE END

Acknowledgements

I would like to thank all my friends and family who encouraged me to not give up on my dream. A special thanks to Barb Poprawa who read draft after draft for me. Andy and Francesca Bohannon - Andy, thanks for always reminding me to write. Francesca for reading the almost final draft. To my sister Vonnie Hiller for keeping me grounded in reality, and for Beth Miller for proofing my final draft and to everyone who purchases my book. Thank you!

The author takes full responsibility for any and all errors.

Cover Design by Kelly Sandula-Gruner

Grunergraphics.com

Made in the USA
Columbia, SC
30 August 2020